CW00850632

The Man of Snow, and Other Tales

Harriet Myrtle

BIBLIOBAZAAR

A VOICE FROM THE SNOW MAN.

THE MAN OF SNOW,

AND OTHER TALES.

BY MRS. HARRIET MYRTLE,

AUTHOR OF "THE PET LAMB," "LITTLE AMY'S BIRTHDAY," ETC.

WITH COLOURED FRONTISPIECE.

LONDON:
FREDERICK WARNE AND CO.,
BEDFORD STREET, COVENT GARDEN.
1867.

CONTENTS.

INTRODUCTION.

THE cottage door is no longer over-hung with roses, clematis, and honeysuckle; the flowers in the garden are dead; there are no daisies in the fields; the trees are leafless; the robin that sang among the bright red berries of the mountain-ash now hops close to the window to ask for a crumb, and whistles his thanks perched on a bare bough.

We have told how little Mary enjoyed

the sweet Spring, the bright Summer, and the breezy Autumn; now we shall find how happy she was in the dreary Winter. In every change and at every time there are beautiful things for those who can see and feel them. Kind hearts can shed a warmth like sunshine, and deeds of love will bring gladness into every season.

THE MAN OF SNOW,

AND OTHER TALES.

WINTER PLEASURES.

DO jump up and look out at the
trees, said Susan, one morning
in December, to little Mary, " they are
so beautiful, all sparkling like silver."

" It seems very cold," said Mary,
rather sleepily. " Will you draw up the
blind, Susan, that I may see out."

Susan drew up the blind. "Oh!"
cried Mary, " how lovely the window

looks! I see fairy palaces, and wreaths of flowers, and numbers of birds, and bright butterflies! Oh! and look at those angels, flying with white wings spread, and below them there is a lovely lake. Look, Susan, do you see what I mean?"

"I don't see that so plain," replied Susan; "but I see a pretty cottage just there, in the corner of this pane."

"Oh, yes!" said Mary; "and look, there is a high mountain behind it, and a forest of tall fir-trees growing all up the sides, and there is a river running along before it, with pretty flowers like stars on its banks. Oh! and little fairies dancing among them; now it all sparkles like diamonds and rubies! Beautiful, beautiful!" cried Mary, jumping out of bed. The sun had just risen, and his beams, tinged with red, shone on little Mary's frosted window, and gave it this beautiful appearance.

"But it is much too cold to stand looking at it, dear," said Susan; "make haste, and let us get you down to the warm parlour fire."

Splash went Mary into her bath, and made all the haste possible; and while she was dressing, the window was a continual pleasure; for as the sun shone on the glass, small portions of the frost-work melted away, and let the bright rays shine through; and first these clear spots looked like little shining stars on the fairies' foreheads; then. like stars in the sky; then they changed into pretty ponds in a wood; then into lakes with rocky banks; the angels seemed to fly farther away; the wreath of flowers took different forms; the fairies danced off with the birds and butterflies; and at last, just as the largest lake had become so large, that Mary thought it must be the sea, it was time to go down stairs.

The parlour looked so very comfortable and felt so warm. There was a bright fire; Bouncer was stretched on the rug; the kettle boiled on the hob;

breakfast was laid : the sun shone in at the lattice window. And now Mary, looking out into the garden, remembered what Susan had said about the trees, for they did indeed look beautiful. Every branch and every twig was encrusted over with crystals of white frost; they no longer appeared like common trees; no wood was to be seen; they seemed to have been changed by some fairy in the night into silver, and sprinkled with diamonds. The laurels and other ever-greens had all their leaves covered and fringed round the edges with the same silvery, sparkling frost-work. The ivy-leaves near the window looked the best of all; their dark green colour seemed to make the jewels shine more brightly, and then their pretty forms were shown off by all this ornament. As Mary was fancying herself in some fairy palace, or in Aladdin's garden, and wondering whether there was any fruit made of precious stones hanging on the trees, her papa and mamma came down to breakfast, and they all enjoyed the sight together. Mary's pretty cousin, Chrissy, who had been May-Queen on the first of May, was on a visit at the cottage, and when she came down, she was delighted too with the beautiful sight, and thought the branches 'te white coral tipped with diamonds.

While they were at breakfast, the fairy scene vanished; for as the warm sun shone on the frost-work, it melted away in drops of water.

" I could fancy the trees were crying," said Mary, " because they are losing their bright jewels."

Her mamma smiled, and told her to look at something new and bright that had come among the ivy-leaves. Mary looked out, and saw a row of shining icicles hanging down, where the dark, thick leaves kept off the heat of the sun ; so that the water, as it melted, had frozen again before it had dropped on the ground.

And now Mary asked the question which she had asked for several mornings past. It was, "Do you think Aunt Mary, and Thomas, and Willie will come to-day ?"

"I think it quite possible that they may," said her mamma; "but to-morrow is more likely."

"You had better try not to expect them till to-morrow, Mary," said Chrissy.

"I will *try*," said Mary, "but I think I do expect them to-day. And now let me think how many days it is before Christmas-eve will come. Yesterday we counted it was eleven days, so to-day it is ten. *Still* ten days."

" But you know, Mary, we have plenty to do, first," said her mamma. Mary nodded and smiled.

Christmas-eve was the day they kept at the cottage; because Mary's papa and mamma always spent Christmas-day with grandmamma. She lived in a large old house, in a country town ten miles off. Everything in her house was clean and shining; the rooms smelt very sweet; and grandmamma was very kind, and let the children do whatever they liked; and her two maids were so good-natured and petted them; and there were always such nice cakes, oranges, and jellies. Then, in the evenings, there was sure to

be a magic lantern, or a man to play the
fiddle; in short, going to grandmamma's
was a very great pleasure.

Mary now asked her papa to come
down to the pond, and give her another
lesson in sliding. He came out, and as
they ran along they found numbers of
things to admire. Every blade of grass
was fringed with the white frost-work,
and the leaves of all the weeds that grew
near the hedges looked quite pretty with
their new trimming. But, above all, the
mosses in the little wood that skirted the
field were most lovely. When winter
strips the trees of their leaves, then the
little, bright green mosses come and

clothe the roots and stems, as if to do all they can to comfort them; and to-day they were sparkling all over, and seemed to be dressed out for some festival. Mary and her papa stopped before a weeping birch-tree, with the green moss growing on its silvery white stem. After admiring it for some time, they looked up at its branches that hung drooping over their heads. "How light and feathery they look," said Mary. "I think they are quite as pretty as in summer."

"I think so, too," said her papa. "I even think the birch more beautiful in winter than in summer; and all the trees show us the grandeur and beauty of their forms more when the leaves are gone.   Look at their great sweeping branches."

" Yes," said Mary, " and then all the little twigs look so pretty, and like lace-work."

" And more than ever we must admire them," said her papa, " when we think that in every little bud at their tips lie the young leaves folded in, and safely shielded by this brown covering from the cold; but all ready to burst forth when the soft spring air and sunshine tell them it is time."

" Mary was delighted at this thought, and they spent a little while looking at different buds, particularly those of the chestnut-trees, with their shining brown coats. Mary took great care not to break one off; she said, "It would be such a pity the little leaves should not feel the spring air, and come out in the sunshine."

"But, oh! Chrissy! what a lovely bunch of jewelled leaves you have collected," cried she. "Oh, yes, that branch in the middle will look pretty; it has managed to go on looking like coral, and to keep its diamonds, because it was so shaded. Now you will put the brown oak leaves, all shining. Here are some more; *do* put these; and then the pretty little brown beech leaves glittering all over. It looks beautiful !"

" How pretty the form of the oak leaves is," said Chrissy.

" Now let us take it in to mamma," cried Mary.

" But, remember," said Chrissy, "if we take it in, all its charm will vanish. Here in the frosty air it looks as if it had been dressed up by the fairies, but in the warm room we should soon have nothing but a bare twig and a few withered leaves."

Mary looked rather sad.

" See," said Chrissy, " let us fasten it to the top of your mamma's favourite seat under the beech tree; it

will make a pretty ornament there."
And so it did, and was much admired;
and shaded as it was, it kept its jewels
on the whole day.

Now the sliding began. Mary's papa
took hold of her hand and ran with her
along the field, till they came to the
edge of the pond; then away they went,
sliding side by side. He kept tight hold
of her hand; for she could not help
tumbling down very often, because this
was only the second time she had tried.
Once they very nearly both had a tumble,
for Bouncer came out, and ran bounding
and barking by their side, and rushed on
the ice with them; but he suddenly

stopped short and barked, as if to say,
" How is this ! what makes the water so
hard this morning?" and when he
stopped they nearly tumbled over him,
but they managed to keep up. After
sliding till Mary's face looked like a rosy-
cheeked apple, it was time to go in to
lessons ; and afterwards they took a walk,
and saw some gentlemen and boys skating on the large pond on the common.

Among the people looking on were
two little boys just come from India,
that warm country. They had never
seen frost, or snow, or ice, and they
could not be persuaded to go upon the
pond; they thought they should cer-

tainly sink. At last a gentleman
caught up the youngest in his arms and
skated away with him, at which the poor
little fellow began to cry. When his
brother saw this, he hurried on the ice,
keeping tight hold of his nurse's hand,
and the gentleman came skating back
with the little one and put him down, so
now they both went on together.

Just as Mary's mamma said they
must go home, the London coach with
its four horses came gaily along the hard
frosty road along the common. A boy
on the top waved a red handkerchief,
and Mary cried out, "That's Thomas, I
know it is!" She was quite right, for

the coach stopped, and aunt Mary and
Willie got out, while Thomas slid down
from the roof. They were soon shaking
hands, giving kisses and kind welcomes,
and all walked merrily up the lane, and
had a very happy dinner.

All the afternoon was spent in talking
over everything that had happened to
everybody since they parted; hearing
Thomas's school adventures; visiting
Cowslip and Primrose, the cow and her
pretty young daughter; Chanticleer and
Partlet, and all their children and rela-
tions; the pigeons and the goats; unpacking boxes, and looking at new books
or toys.

Then came what Mary called " happy time." This was the time when it grew dark, candles were brought, shutters and curtains closed, and they all collected round the tea-table, while the fire blazed, the kettle boiled, and everything looked bright and pleasant. This evening it seemed happier than ever; and next morning it was delightful to awake and remember who had come to the cottage, and to see the party at breakfast; and then to have Thomas-and Willie to slide on the pond. Mary grew quite a brave slider before they were called in to dinner.

When dinner was over, she asked her

mamma whether they should not go on with nice work this evening? and her mamma said, "Oh, yes, they must, or they should not be ready." This "nice work" was preparing a number of presents, which were to be given away at Christmas. None of their friends had been forgotten. Mary was busy hemming, knitting, dressing dolls, and making pincushions; her mamma was also hard at work, and besides, was often cutting out and fixing, and had a village girl, who came almost every day for work, making frocks and different things; Chrissy was also busy making all kinds ℓ pretty things.

When Aunt Mary heard of it, she said, "We are all at work in the same way. Thomas has brought his turning lathe, and a few tools that he has, and he and Willie are very busy about something." Thomas put his finger on his lips to show her that she must not tell what that something was, and Willie put his arms round her neck, and whispered something very mysteriously.

"Chrissy and Mary have some secret too," said Mary's mamma; "they go into a room by themselves every day, and nobody must disturb them."

At this they both laughed.

"Well, we shall know about it all on

Christmas-eve," said Mary, "and then, besides, we shall see somebody, mamma says; somebody that is coming here that we shall like very much, and that we know, and yet have never seen."

"Is it a gentleman or lady?" asked Thomas.

"A gentleman," said Mary, "I have guessed everybody I can think of, but I cannot find out."

"Somebody we know and yet have never seen," said Thomas; "who can it be?"

THE MAN OF SNOW.

NOW then, dear mamma, said Mary, "do tell us the story you promised us when we were out walking to-day, about the Man of Snow! I so long to hear about him."

"But he was not a real man?" said Willie.

"No, to be sure not," answered Mary's mamma; "he was only a figure of snow, made in something like the shape of a man."

" And could he walk?" said Willie.

" No, he had no proper legs. His broad legs were both joined together, and his arms lay flat to his broad sides."

" Ha! ha! ha!" laughed Thomas ; " he was rather a clumsy man."

" But how did he come?" inquired Willie, very earnestly.

" How was the man made, mamma?" asked Mary. " Who made the figure?"

" I will tell you all about it," said her mamma.

" Bouncer," said Mary, " move a little farther on the rug, will you, so that I may sit at mamma's feet, near Willie ; but when the story gets very interesting indeed, I shall be obliged to come and sit on mamma's knee, opposite to Willie."

" Now," said Willie; and Mary's mamma thus began :—

" When I was a little girl, about the age of Mary, we lived entirely in the country for several years, and one winter there was a great fall of snow. The snow covered the roof of the house, and the roofs of the stable and cow-house; and the branches of every tree were so thickly covered with the beautiful white snow, that sometimes in the morning, when I was being dressed, and looked out of the window, I could at first have fancied the trees were all apple and pear-

trees full of blossoms. You may, therefore, suppose that the snow lay very
deep in the fields.

"We had three fields; one was ad-
joining our kitchen-garden; and there
was often a cow, horse, or pony allowed
to walk about in it when the grass was
good.   This field sloped down into a
second, which was parted off by a gate;
and then, by a pathway along the side of
a high hedge, we came to a stile, and on
the other side of the stile was our largest
field.   No cattle were allowed to enter
this field, as it was kept entirely for grass
to make hay with.   Here, then, the deep
snow lay, all broad and white, and soft,

and without the marks of a single foot-step all over the whole bright expanse, where all was whiteness and silence, and where nothing was moving.

"Now, there lived in a pretty lane very near us an old parish-clerk, named Downes. He lived in his cottage alone, excepting his little granddaughter and a blackbird. He was a tall, thin old man, with straight white hair; very kind to all the children, but had a long face, and was very serious. His name was Godfrid, but we always called him Gaffer Downes.

"One morning, during this great snow time, Mr. Gaffer Downes came to my father, and asked permission to make

something curious in his large field.
He explained what it was, and had leave
given him directly; for everybody was fond
of Gaffer Downes. He had been parish-
clerk in our village nearly forty years.

" Away went Mr. Downes to get
assistants for what he wished to do, and
he soon found two who were willing to
help him.   One was the coachman of
Squire Turner's family, who were neighbours and friends of ours ; and the other
was the parish sexton and cow-doctor.
It was a particular part of the sexton's
duty to keep all the tombstones clear of
weeds with his spade, and also to attend
to the ivy that grew up the church walls,

just to prevent it from covering up the windows. He brought his spade with him; and the three went trudging off together through the snow.

" They took their way down into our great field, and there they each made a snow-ball. Following the directions of Gaffer Downes, these snow-balls were rolled along until they collected more and more snow upon their sides, all round, and of course began to get very large. Each man's snow-ball was soon as large as his head. They went rolling on, and soon each of the snow-balls was as large as two heads; then as large as a cow's head; then as large as a very great cow's head; and then each man was obliged to stop, as he could roll his snow-ball along no more, it was so large and heavy."

"Oh! how I should have liked to have been there to help," cried Thomas.

"Mr. Downes then told the coachman and the sexton to leave their snowballs and come and help him to roll his. So all three pushed away, and rolled it nearly all round the great field, by which time it was as large as the head of an elephant. They stopped to rest and take breath. They were all very warm, and the sexton was so hot, he was obliged to take off his coat as he had underneath it an old red waistcoat, of thick cloth, with sleeves made out of a pair of worsted stockings with the feet cut off. Mr. Downes now informed them that he wished this large ball to be rolled to the middle of the field, and to remain there while they rolled the others to the same size, and then brought them to the same spot. They were just beginning their work again, when they heard a loud merry laugh at the other side of the hedge, and who should they see looking over, and showing his white teeth, and making a funny face at them, but George Poole, the black footman at Squire Turner's.

"'Aha!' said George, 'aha, Massa Down, me see you! how you do, Massa Gaffer Down? and how you do, you lilly pretty granddaughter at home? and how you do, you blackbird, Massa Down? aha! very fond of blacky bird, he just my colour. How you do, you cold finger, Massa Gaffer Down, and Massa sexton and coachyman too, with cold fingers, all so red, like scraped carrot.'"

"'George Poole,' said Mr. Downes, with a serious look, 'George Poole, you interrupt, come and assist us, or return home to your fire in a quiet and proper manner, I beg of you.'"

"'Me go home to proper fire,' answered George, 'but what you make there with great big snow-ball, Massa Down?'"

" 'I do not intend to let any one know at present,' answered Mr. Downes; 'good day, George;' and as he said this, he made a sign to the coachman and sexton, and they continued their work of rolling.

" 'Me come and see him when him finished,' said George, 'good day, Massa Down;' and as he said this, the laughing black face of George Poole disappeared from the top of the hedge."

" What made George Poole speak so funnily?" asked Willie.—" He was not an Englishman, but a negro," answered

Mary's mamma. " The negroes have a language of their own, and seldom learn to speak English quite rightly

" This work of rolling continued all the morning, and as they found they had nothing else to do, they worked at it all the afternoon also. By this time they had made seven balls of snow, each as large as the head of an elephant, and had rolled them all into the very middle of the field. But to do this, they had been obliged to ask for the help of two men from our house. This my father readily gave; indeed, I believe he himself helped at the last rolling of each ball, as they were so very heavy, and moved so slowly.

Mr. Downes then took the spade and patted every ball with the flat part of it, in order to make them even and hard, and so left them for the night.

" The next morning, while we were at breakfast, Gaffer Downes passed by the window with a spade over his shoulder, followed by the sexton and the coachman, each with a spade over his shoulder; and after them came the beadle, the church bell-ringer, and the young man who blew the bellows for the organ. They all followed Mr. Downes into the large field.

"Up we all jumped from the break-fast-table, and hurried on our things; papa, and mamma, and I and Ellen

Turner, who had heard of something that was to be done in our field, and had come over to breakfast with us to see. Away we all went, mamma, carrying me where the snow was too deep, and papa carrying Ellen Turner.

" When we came into the large field, there we saw them all very busy indeed, working under the directions of Gaffer Downes, who was not working himself now, but standing still in the attitude of an artist giving orders to his pupils. They soon made a sort of flat bank of snow, about a foot and a half high, and patted it down very hard with their spades. The ' pupils,' that is to say the coachman, and sexton, and bell-ringer, and beadle, and the young man who blew the bellows for the organ, then rolled three of the great balls of snow up on this bank close to each other, so as to form a sort of circle, but leaving a hollow place in the middle, of the form of a triangle, which the beadle remarked was very much the figure of the coachman's Sunday hat. Mr. Downes now came with his spade and made this three-cornered hollow larger, in fact large enough for a man to stand in very easily. He then desired the coachman and sexton to assist him with their spades in making the tops of these three balls quite flat. When this was done, he directed them to make three more of the balls flat at top and bottom. This also being done, he called all his party together, and told them to lift these last three balls, one at a time, and carefully place them upon the top of those three that were already placed, as I have told you. So the pupils did as they were directed, and then Mr. Downes made three notches like steps in the side of two of the balls, and up them he slowly walked with his spade, and again made the three-cornered hole in the middle of the three top snow-balls, as large as he had made it in those at the bottom. We all thought he was going to get into it, but he did not, he only looked in.

" He now came down with a very important look, and went up to the one large ball of snow, which still lay there in its round shape. This he trimmed and patted all about into the form he wished, and then all the pupils were called to carry it, and lift it by degrees to place at the very top, where it was intended to be made the head of a Man of Snow. It was a great job to get the head safely up, it was so very heavy. However, after much time, and many narrow escapes of the head and all the pupils tumbling down together, they did manage to get it up to the top, just over the hole, which it covered up, and its own weight kept it there safely. It was now time to go to dinner. We all went, but we finished as soon as we could, and returned to the large field. Gaffer Downes, the coachman, and sexton, moved round and round with their spades, cutting and shaving, or patting up the snow to make the figure of the Man. And as there were several hollow places where you could look into the inside, they filled them up with hard lumps of snow, all except one hole, which Mr. Downes said he wished left open to let in air, though, on second thoughts, he said he would cover it over himself, and so he did, but very lightly. They made a few trenches and ridges down the middle and at the sides of the Man, and this they called his legs and arms, at which we all laughed. Lastly, Mr. Downes went climbing up the sides with his spade, and went to work at the head. What he tried to do was to make a face to it, but it was very difficult. He cut out the nose and chin very large and broad; but some unlucky cut, just as he was finishing, made them fall off. He then asked the beadle to bring him two short sticks from the hedge; this being done, he stuck them into the face, and covered them over with handfuls of snow, which he pressed and patted into the shape of a nose and a chin. But when he had finished, the weight of the snow made the sticks come out, and down they fell. He went on trying again and again, and we all looked on and hoped he would succeed, though we laughed very much also, for the nose fell off six times, and the chin four. At last, however, with a sudden thought, which could only have occurred to one who had quite a genius for making a Man of Snow—Mr. Downes stuck the two short sticks in, not pointing downwards or straight out, but pointing rather upwards, so that the weight of the nose and chin were supported upon the face, and then held fast. And a very strange face it was!

"Two things were still to be done. Mr. Downes drew from his coat pocket a couple of large round stones, of a blue grey colour, and these he fixed in the face for the eyes; and over the head, and at each side, he stuck a number of small hedge twigs, and a wreath from a thorny wild rose-tree, for hair. If more snow should fall, he assured us the hair would look quite beautiful."

"I hope some snow *would* fall," said Mary.

"Down came Mr. Gaffer Downes, looking so seriously and modestly upon the snow-clumps on his shoes, while we all praised his work, and told him how much we liked his Man of Snow. It was now evening; we all went back through the fields, and when we arrived at the house, my papa sent out a quantity of hot ale with sugar and toast in it for the pupils, and we made Mr. Downes come in to tea with us, though he wanted to go home, as he said his little granddaughter and the blackbird would think he was lost in the snow.

"There did happen to be a light fall of snow again in the night, and we all

went down to the large field next morning after breakfast to see what change it
had made in the appearance of the great
Man. And a fine change indeed it had
made. He looked much larger, and
rounder, and whiter, and colder, and
seemed more 'at home' in the great
white field. And he had a wonderful
head of hair!"

"But," said Thomas, "one thing I
do not understand; why did Mr. Downes
make the Man of Snow hollow inside like
the trunk of a hollow tree? It could not
be for air. What need was there for
any air?"

"And why," asked Mary, "did he

leave a great hole open, or very lightly covered at one side? was that for air too?"

"Did the negro blacky, George Poole, come and see the 'Man of Snow' when he was finished?" asked Willie.

"You will know, or guess all in time," answered Mary's mamma. "And now, Mary, come and sit upon my knee, for the most interesting part of the story is coming."

Up jumped Mary, and gave Willie a kiss, who was on the opposite knee; her mamma thus continued—

"The very same evening as we were all sitting round the fire about half an

hour before supper-time, Mr. Downes
came to our house, and sent in word
that he had something very important
to say. Mamma said, 'Pray tell Mr.
Downes to come in directly.' In came
Gaffer Downes, looking rather paler
than usual, and with his face looking
longer than usual, and his white hair
looking straighter than usual, and his
chin sticking out with some frost upon
it. He remained standing in the middle
of the room without saying a word.

"'What is the matter, Mr. Downes?'
said papa.

"'Sir,' said Mr. Downes, without moving from the place where he stood, 'some-

thing has happened.'—'What has happened?' said papa, rising from his chair.

" 'An event!' answered Mr. Downes.

" 'What event?' said mamma, rising
from her chair; 'and where has it happened?'—'In the large field,' answered
Mr. Gaffer Downes. 'An event has
happened to the "Man of Snow!"' '

" At this we all ran up to Gaffer
Downes, exclaiming, 'What has happened to him—tell us at once.' "

" Oh! I hope the Man of Snow had
not tumbled down," cried Mary.—"You
shall hear," said her mamma.

" 'The Man,' said Mr. Downes in a
low voice—' the Man talks.'

" ' Talks ! ' cried we all.

"'Yes,' said he, 'the Man speaks. He was addressing the field in a long speech when I passed on the other side of the hedge. It is a fine moonlight night, you can all come and hear him yourselves.'

" ' That we will,' exclaimed my papa, ' we will all go directly.'

" So mamma called for bonnets, and shawls, and handkerchiefs, and cloaks, and muffs, and tippets, and gloves, and fur boots, and all sorts of things, for there were several young ladies staying on a visit with us. And outside the door we found Squire Turner's coachman, with the sexton and beadle, and bell-ringer, and the young man who blew the bellows for the organ; in fact all Gaffer Downes' 'pupils' waiting to go with us into the large field.

"Off we all set, Mr. Downes leading the way. At the end of the first field, he made us all stop to listen. He asked us if any of us could hear the 'Man of Snow' speaking. We all listened, and at last said 'No.' He then told us to follow him slowly along by the hedge of the second field, listening all the way. We heard nothing; and again Mr. Downes stopped us all at the stile leading into the great field. Very attentively we listened; but all was as silent as possible.

"Mr. Downes now told us we had better wait a little, and let him go first, and as soon as the Man of Snow spoke he would return and tell us to come softly. So over the stile got Mr. Downes, and we soon lost sight of him, as he went creeping round close by the hedge.

"Well, we waited and waited, but Mr. Downes did not return. We listened; but we could hear nothing. Still we waited; but at last papa got out of patience, and said, 'What can have become of Mr. Downes?' 'I hope,' said mamma, 'nothing has happened to him.' 'I am determined,' said papa, 'to go and see after him.'—'Let us all go to-gether,' said mamma. 'Let us all go together straight up towards the Man of Snow, and ask after Mr. Downes?'

"It was agreed upon, and we all got over the stile, and went crowding to-gether along the field, nobody liking to go first, but all keeping close like sheep when they do not know what to do for the best.

"At last we came near the great Man of Snow. Papa, and the young man who blew the bellows for the organ, stood in front; and next to them the sexton; and then mamma with all us girls clinging close round her, wrapped up in our cloaks, with only our eyes and noses to be seen; and behind us stood the rest of the pupils; and behind all, at some distance, stood the beadle.

" Well, there we all stood in silence, in the great silent snow field, looking at the great silent Man of Snow, with the moon shining upon his head!

" The young man who blew the bellows for the organ was the first who spoke; and he said in a very respectful voice, ' I ask your pardon, sir—but *could* you be so kind as to tell us what has become of Mr. Downes ? '

" No answer was returned. Everything was as silent as before.

"The sexton now spoke; and in a very humble tone he said, 'May it please your Majesty!—we have lost the clerk of the parish!'

"Again we all remained in the same suspense and silence. The moon now went partly behind a cloud, so that only a little pale light came across one side of the head and shoulders of the Man of Snow. At last papa was obliged to speak, and he said,—

"Oh, Man of Snow! we come not to disturb thy tranquillity; but if·thy gracious Whiteness hath once already spoken to these fields, permit us also to hear thy solemn voice!'

" There was again a pause, and then —would you believe it?—you hardly can—would you believe it—the Man of Snow answered! He did indeed ; in a very slow and solemn voice he said,—

" ' Peace be upon ye all—and the silent thoughtfulness of these white fields.' You may suppose how fearful and astonished, and quiet we all stood, at hearing these words. Presently, however, my papa took courage, and again addressed the Man of Snow.

" ' Who art thou—and whence comest thou, oh, most serene Highness of the Frost ? '

" ' I am a spirit of Winter !' answered

the Man of Snow, in the same solemn tone. 'Once I was alive, and had a large body. In Lapland I was one of the most renowned giants. There my image is built up with white stone. And because this likeness of me has here been made, therefore on the wings of the wind hath my spirit crossed the bleak seas, to dwell for a little time in this body of snow. But now depart!—I would be alone!—Retire!—To-morrow, at moonrise ye may come again.'

"We did not dare to disobey this command to depart, you may be sure; so we all went homewards, too full of thoughts to speak.

" Just as we had reached the stile, one of the young ladies cried out ' Oh, what's that under the hedge ?' We all looked, and there we saw the head of a man rising out of the dry ditch by the side of the hedge ! Who do you think it was ? it was the poor beadle ! he had been so frightened when the Man of Snow spoke, that he had run back, but being unable to get over the stile in his confusion, he got into the dry ditch, and sat there upon the dead leaves and snow, with his chin just level with the top of the bank. However, the pupils soon lifted him out, and comforted him, and took him home. They also went to the cottage of Gaffer Downes, to know if he had returned safely.   But he had not.

" Before we went to supper, however, we sent to the cottage, as we were getting very anxious; and his granddaughter answered from the window, that her dear grandfather had returned, and had a basin of warm broth, and was now in bed.

" We could hardly eat our supper, any of us, for talking of the Man of Snow, and what he had said about having been once upon a time a Lapland giant! For my part, I could not sleep for thinking of it; and all the young ladies said the same the next morning at breakfast.

" You may be sure we were all very

anxious for the evening to come, when we were again to go and hear what the Man of Snow had to say. He told us, you recollect, to come again at moon-rise; and the moon, papa said, would rise about seven o'clock.

"We had a dinner-party at our house, and nearly all the time we talked of little else except the Man of Snow, or rather what he had done when he was a giant in Lapland; and we thought that perhaps he might tell us the history of his life. We determined, every one of us, to go all together down to the great field, when the moon rose.

"As the time approached we became

so anxious that we got ready too soon,
and then as we were all ready, we thought
we might just as well go, and wait
there till the white giant chose to speak.

" So off we all set, and went very
merrily, and yet not without some little
fears, down towards the large field.

" But when we had all got over the
stile, who should come running and
calling after us, but Mr. Downes.   He
was quite out of breath ; but as soon as
he could speak, he said, ' Indeed you
are too soon !   It is too soon by half an
hour !   You had much better get over
the stile again, and go into the other
·ld a little while !'

"Now this made some of us laugh; for, do you know, we *now* began to suspect that it was Mr. Downes himself who had spoken for the Man of Snow."—"Do you know, mamma," whispered Mary, " that is just what I have been thinking too."—"Yes to be sure," said Thomas, " and that was why he left the hollow place and the hole."

"What! did he get inside the Man of Snow and speak?" said Willie. " But go on, mamma," cried Mary.

"We thought perhaps he had got behind somewhere, or perhaps into the inside of the great figure, and thus spoken for him. But now as we had come too

soon, he had no time to get ready. We
were sorry for poor Gaffer Downes, yet
still we could not help laughing at the
scrape he was in. He went on assuring
us the Man of Snow would not speak at
all, as we had come before the time he
ordered. But this made us laugh the
more, as we were now almost sure how
it had been contrived.

"Meantime we had slowly advanced
towards the Man of Snow; poor Mr.
Downes telling us all the time that the
man would be sure not to utter a word,
as we had disobeyed his directions.

"'But see!' said papa, 'the moon is
now rising!'

" ' Ah, 'tis no matter now ;' answered Mr. Downes, in a melancholy tone. ' The Man of Snow will not speak a single word.'

" Mr. Downes had scarcely said this, when a voice from the Man of Snow called out in a loud tone—

" ' How you do, Massa Down !—how you lilly granddaughter do—and how you do you blackbird, Massa Gaffer Down ? '

" We instantly all burst into a fit of laughter."

It was some time before the story could go on, for Mary laughed so much, that she jumped down off her mamma's knee. Thomas laughed still louder, and

Willie kept saying, "But how was it?" At last they were able to listen again.

"All laughed very much," continued Mary's mamma, "except poor Mr. Downes, who walked backwards and forwards once or twice, saying, 'Dear me! how very vexatious!'

"Papa and mamma now both went up to Mr. Downes, and told him they saw how vexed he was at the change that had somehow or other taken place in the voice of the Man of Snow, because the spirit of the Lapland giant had certainly flown away, and quite a different one had got into its place. However, they begged him not to take it to heart, but to go and speak to the Man of Snow, and ask him to explain a little.

"Mr. Downes thought for a minute, and then seeming to make up his mind to it, walked a few paces nearer to the Man of Snow, and this curious dialogue took place between them :—

"MR. DOWNES. 'Who art thou, oh, rude familiar voice, who hast usurped the place of the frosty Spirit of last night?'

"MAN OF SNOW. 'Me the King of Lapland!—speaky more respectful to him Snow-ball Majesty, Massa Down!'

"MR. DOWNES. 'No Majesty of Snow hast thou, nor art thou Lapland's king; nor ever wert, nor shalt be.'

" MAN OF SNOW. 'Why you say so, you Massa Gaffer man! Me come from own country Lapland late last night, after supper.'

"MR. DOWNES. 'What then for supper did the King of Lapland eat?'

" MAN OF SNOW. 'Berry good supper to be sure—great supper in great big palace, surrounded with orange trees, and plantain, and banana trees. Me have curried chicken plenty, and hot rice, with treacle, and a pine-apple, and water-melon from own gardens close by; and then me have chocolate, berry sweet, and great big cigar to smoke! What 'ou tink now, Massa Down?'

"MR. DOWNES. 'I think the King of Lapland dreams.'

"MAN OF SNOW. 'What he dream of, then?'

"MR. DOWNES. 'He dreams that he had supper in some West Indian isle; for in Lapland no oranges, no pines, no melons grow, no plantain, no banana.'

"MAN OF SNOW. 'Me never say they did grow there.'

"When the Man of Snow said this, we all of us together cried out, 'Oh! oh!' meaning, what a story he was telling.

"MAN OF SNOW. 'Me never mean to say so. Me have great big hot-house, all glass, where fruit grow; and other ting me have brought over in fine large ship. Me very rich king; hab everything me wish.'

"MR. DOWNES. 'Rich, dost thou say! in money or in land?'

"MAN OF SNOW. 'In money to be sure. Me have large chest full of dollars— Lapland dollars; and guineas too—my friend and brother, King of England, send me; and me have plenty land too. Large fields of rice—no, not rice—rice not grow in Lapland—me know dat very well—me mean to say, large plantation of sugar-cane.'

"MR. DOWNES. 'Nor doth the sugar-cane in Lapland grow.'

"MAN OF SNOW. 'Me know that very well—me just going to say so. But me *try* to make him grow; me try to bring new tings into my country; me try to get horses, and oxen, and sheep, and deer, and dogs, and nanny goats, into my kingdom, and send away bull-frogs, and rattle snakes. Me want to change scorpions and mosquetoes into butter-flies and lady-birds. Me want to have all manner fine houses for fine birds— parrots, and maccaws, with green wings, and scarlet tails, and blue breasts, and top-knots; and peacocks, and birds of paradise, and a great pond for gold and silver fishes. And me mean to build great big bamboo houses for all these, twice as high as my head.'

"As the Man of Snow said this, we all saw his head shake a little, as if he was in a great fuss with what he was thinking of doing; and we even thought we saw the upper part of the figure shake a little, and some pieces of snow begin to crumble and fall. But he went on speaking again.

"Man of Snow. 'And me mean to have elephants, and rhinoceroses, and apes, with long arms and blue noses. And me mean to build a house for elephants, very large and very strong; so that when we catch wild elephant he no can get out. He try and try—but he can't.'—Here we all saw the Man of Snow shake again.

"MAN OF SNOW. 'Makey house all sides very strong bamboo. See him angry trunk poke through the bars of cage—but all too fast and strong. He no *can* get out. Then he make trumpet noise with trunk, and him lilly cunning eye look so very angry; and then he run him head right against the front of cage to try and push him down! but it all too strong and he can't!—yet he push!—and push!—and trumpet with trunk—and scream—and push! and oh, Massa Down!——'

" As the Man of Snow uttered these words, off rolled his head, and broke into twenty pieces !—and the next instant the whole figure cracked, and opened in the middle, and fell to pieces—and out rolled the black man, George Poole, upon the snow, crying out, 'Oh, Massa Down, why you no build him stronger ?'

" You may suppose how we all laughed. One of the young ladies almost went into a fit with laughing, and most of us laughed till we had a pain at both sides of the face, and yet we were unable to stop. Even Mr. Downes laughed ; not at first, though, it first he made a very long face ; then he began '*te! he! he!*'—and '*he! he! he!*' till at last he went into 'ha! ha! ha! oh, dear me!'—and was obliged to sit down upon the snow and wipe his forehead to recover himself.

"We all returned to the house very merrily, laughing all the way. We brought the King of Lapland with us, for George had always been a favourite in the village; so we told the cook to give his Majesty a large basin of rice, milk, and sugar, and mamma sent him afterwards a large slice of plum cake, and a tumbler with port wine and lemon, to make negus. Papa requested Mr. Downes to come in to supper with us, but he said that he really must go home, as his granddaughter and the blackbird would think something had happened to him. Papa, however, would take no denial, so we made Mr. Downes come in, and then we sent a man for his granddaughter, with a message that she was to bring the blackbird with her.

" So, in a few minutes afterwards, in came a pretty little girl of ten years of age, with blue eyes and flaxen hair, and a complexion like a rose, bringing in her hand a large milk-white wicker cage, with the blackbird sitting in the middle. He was as black as a coal, with a yellow bill, and, oh! such a bright black eye. He sat on his perch, with his head bent on one side a little while, then he jumped down to the bottom of the cage, and poking his head out between the bars, gave a good look all round. He then hopped back into the middle of his cage, bowed very low, and very quickly, several times, and then hopped upon his perch, with his tail towards us, but instantly whisked round, as if he was afraid somebody was going to touch his tail. Then he began to sing; he sang nearly all supper-time, and flapped his black wings, while we all stood up and drank the health of Mr. Gaffer Downes, the artist who had made the Man of Snow."

"The *only* thing I wish," said little Mary, "is that George Poole had not broken the Man of Snow."

"You see," said Thomas, "he jumped about, and pushed with his head like the elephant, and that was the reason of the misfortune."

"If I had been there," said Willie, "I should have called out as *loud* as I could—'Take care, negro blacky George Poole, and don't push so hard!'"

"Well, at any rate," said Mary, "he would have melted when it grew warmer; but still, I wish the great silent Man of Snow had not been broken to pieces. He must have looked so grand, standing in the great silent snow field, with the moon shining on his head."

"I like that funny George Poole so much!" cried Willie.

" So do I," said Thomas.

" Yes, and so do I, too," cried Mary; "he even made that grave Gaffer Downes laugh. But I like the blackbird *so* much, hopping about and bowing; I know exactly how he went on. And then the little granddaughter; what was her name, mamma?"

" Her name," answered her mamma, " was little Susie Downes. But now it is bed-time."

So they all went to bed, and little Mary dreamed all night of the Man of Snow, and of the moonlight resting on his head and his silvery white hair.

CHRISTMAS-EVE AT THE COTTAGE.

———◦◦⚬◦◦———

THE ten days that Mary thought of as so long, had passed quickly away and Christmas-eve was come. Two happy days came together—to-day at nome, to-morrow at grand-mamma's; and, besides, Susan, who was to stay at home, was to have a Christmas party, and her father and mother were coming from London to see her.

It was about two hours after break-

fast; the parlour was all put in order
as for a holiday; there were no lessons
nor work about; the fire burned brightly
with a large log upon it; a tall glass
stood on the table, filled with holly-
branches, with splendid red berries, and
mistletoe. Susan had stuck sprigs of
holly in the kitchen window; she was
very busy, assisted by the village girl
who had helped to work, preparing
dinner for to-day and to-morrow; and
besides, making several plum-puddings,
and getting ready dishes of beef, laid on
potatoes, to be sent to the baker's in the
morning for Christmas dinners for some
of their neighbours. Mary's mamma

said she liked them all to have a good dinner on that day.

The spare room was put ready for the gentleman that was expected. Who could he be? They had never guessed. Mary, with Chrissy's assistance, had put into her papa's study all the presents which were to be given away to-day; no one was to go in there till twelve o'clock.

Now came Mary's mamma and papa, and aunt Mary into the parlour. Then Chrissy came; they all sat down by the fire and began to talk, but soon there was a silence. It was certain that they were expecting somebody; the children became quiet too, and listened. It was not long before a ring came at the gate, and Susan was heard showing some one in. Mary's papa and mamma went quickly to the door and brought in a gentleman. They seemed very glad to see him, and he looked so happy and so did aunt Mary and Chrissy. He said quickly, "Is this little Mary?" she held out her hand to him, but looked grave, for she thought to herself, "I do *not* know him;" then he shook hands with the boys and said, " So these are Thomas and Willie." They too thought to themselves, "We do *not* know him." But he looked very good-natured, and they thought, "We should *like* to know him."

A man now came to the door with a portmanteau and carpet bag, which were carried up to the gentleman's room; and then he took off his great coat and sat down, and drew Mary towards him and said to her mamma, "How this dear child reminds me of you when we used to play so many games together, and run over that bright green meadow." Then he seated Mary on his knee, and asked her "if she had got a kite?"

"It's James White! it's James White!" cried Mary, clapping her hands.

" Master James White," exclaimed Thomas—" turned into a gentleman," added little Willie.— " That it is," cried he, laughing heartily ; and in a minute Mary was mounted on one shoulder, Willie on the other, Thomas had hold of his hand, and all four were dear friends directly.

"He is Mr. White now," said Thomas. This made everybody laugh.

" And do you remember making that large new kite ?" said Mary. " On scientific principles," added her mamma. " And flying it," said Thomas, " when it pulled you all three down the meadow slope ?"—"And stuck in a tree," said

Willie.—"Yes, and knocked down five little rooks among the apples and gingerbread," said James White.

At these words, which showed that he was the real maker and flyer of the kite, fresh bursts of joy and laughter began. When quiet was a little restored, James White had some refreshments after his journey, and there was much talk about old times, and about distant countries into which he had travelled, but presently the clock struck twelve.

The sound reminded the children of the room full of presents; and it was a great pleasure to hear Mary's mamma ask their new friend to come into the next room with all of them. Chrissy went first and threw open the door, and they went in. Mary kept fast hold of her mamma's hand, and then ran to her papa and led him to his writing table. " What kind fairy has made me this pretty shaded green rug for my inkstand?" said he. " That kind fairy was mamma," said Mary. " And who has given me this new blotting book, with a beautiful landscape painted on each cover ? ah, Chrissy! I think this must be your doing."—" Yes, and is it not lovely ?" said Mary.

" And here I have found a very pretty bronze taper," said he.—" Aunt Mary gave you that," said Mary; "and don't you like those pretty matches, all twisted up of different coloured paper? Dear little Willie made them."

"Dear little fellow," said her papa, stroking Willie's curly hair; "and here I think I have found some of Thomas's work?"—"Yes," said Mary, "he made that nice little box with his turning-lathe; it is to hold your wafers."

"And who made this pretty pen-wiper? and who hemmed this nice white silk handkerchief, with this bright blue border?" Mary answered by jumping up round his neck, and giving him a kiss.

"How glad I am to see your neat

work, my dear little girl," said he.
" Thank you, and thank you all."

" Now, Aunt Mary dear, open that
work-basket, it is for you," said little
Mary. She opened it; everything was
complete in it. Mamma had chosen the
basket; Chrissy had lined it with rose-
coloured silk, and made the needle-book;
Mary had made the pincushion; papa
had provided the scissors and thimble;
Thomas had turned a neat box to hold
reels of cotton; Willie had made a pretty
little green silk bag, with violet strings,
" to hold buttons or anything mamma
liked." His mamma was quite delighted
with her presents.

Beside the work-basket, there lay on the table a small sealed packet, directed "For the stranger we expect to-day." "Mr. White, James White! that we knew and yet had never seen, this is for you," cried Mary. He broke the seals, and found a purse of dark blue silk, thickly mixed with little steel beads. "Oh! what kind hearts I have come back to," he cried; "thank you all, and particularly the maker of this beautiful purse."

"It was Chrissy that made it," said Mary.—"And I think she is a very kind Chrissy then," said he.

"Now look under the table, Thomas,"

cried Chrissy. Thomas looked down, and saw a box, on the lid of which his own name was written, with the words, "A present from all." He raised the lid. Oh! what a happy boy he was! It was a box of carpenter's tools; everything he had wished for so long was there—hammer, saw, planes, chisels, bradawls, gimlets, screwdrivers, nails, screws, and tacks. He had made nice things before, with the few tools he had, but now, how he should work! "Oh! thank you, thank you all!" he cried, springing up, and running from one to the other. Willie and Mary began to dance together for joy, at seeing him so happy; and as they danced Mary led Willie up to an arm-chair by the fire, and told him to look behind it. He went down on his knees, and crawled behind the chair. Presently out he came dragging by a string a carrier's horse and cart, on the back of which was written "Willie, Carrier." Willie immediately called out, "Wo, Meg!" which made everybody laugh, for he said it so like John, the carrier.

"Papa chose this very horse because it was so like Meg, and had a white face; and look, Willie! these little baskets are hampers; Chrissy painted them brown to look like hampers; you can pack them as you like, they *will* open; and you must pretend these white sacks are full of flour: it's sand you know, but you must pretend."

" Did *you* make them ?" said Willie. " Yes," answered Mary; "and Thomas made the wooden boxes, and they will open too, and you can nail them up with little tacks."—" And cord them with string," said Thomas.

" So I can," cried Willie, looking into one of the boxes, "and put all sorts of things in them."—" And do you see John, the carrier, sitting in front ? Aunt Mary dressed him, is he not like ? Chrissy painted his red face," said Mary.—" And

Mary knit him this blue comforter, exactly like the one she knit for the real John, the carrier;" said Chrissy. "It's lying on the table there; you see they are exactly alike."

"But there is written on the cart, 'Willie, carrier,'" said Willie, looking grave.

"So there is," said, Mary, "what shall we do? we never thought of that."

"We must get Chrissy to alter it," said Thomas, "she can paint John *and* Willie, carriers."

This seemed to satisfy them all, and Willie, after making Meg trot round the room, declared that he liked his cart very much indeed, clapped his hands, gave a shout, and then jumped up into his mamma's arms. " Now Mary is to shut her eyes," he cried.

" Yes," cried Thomas, " shut your eyes, Mary."

Mary hid her face in her mamma's lap. A great deal of whispering and running about went on. " May I look yet," asked Mary, two or three times.

" Now," cried Thomas and Willie, both at once. Mary looked up, and saw at her side, a little table covered with green, on which were feeding about twenty pretty white sheep, and ten lambs; behind them was a sheep fold, a farm-house with green trees about it, four cows, three horses, some pigs, two dogs and a puppy, a milk-maid, and a shepherd playing on a pipe.

"Oh, how *pretty*," cried Mary.

"They are for you," said little Willie. And Thomas whispered to her that Willie had saved all the money that anybody had given him for six months, to buy them. "Dear, kind, little Willie," said Mary, almost crying as she kissed him. "Look, this shall be the farm-house, in the story of 'The Little Milk-Maid,'" said she, "and this shall be Sally."

"And here are Brindle, Dapple, Frisky, and Maggie," said Willie, "and all this, where the sheep are, shall be the field."

" Oh, and this shall be the little dog, Trusty," said Mary, "and we can make this bit of fold into a stile, and Sally can get over it, and we must pretend she has got a pail on her head."

" I will make you a little pail," said Thomas.

"Oh, how nice," cried Willie and Mary, both at once.

" Now look on the other side, Mary," said her mamma. On the other side Mary saw a box of wooden bricks, made for her by Thomas.

" Oh, thank you," cried Mary

have so often wished for bricks, I shall like so very much to build."

"Now turn round, dear Mary," said her papa. In the window was a stand of flowers; two large geraniums, a white and a scarlet, a myrtle, a camellia full of buds, and a heath; on a label, tied to the myrtle, was written, "For our dear little girl, from her papa and mamma." On a lower shelf were two pots of hyacinths and two of narcissi from Aunt Mary, and in the middle a fairy rose in full bloom from Chrissy.

Little Mary looked at the beautiful plants with delight; she kissed them, and stroked the green leaves with her hands; then ran and threw her arms round the kind friends who had given them to her; then she looked rather grave, and said, "But I have got too many things."

"No, no," cried Thomas and Willie.

"Oh, yes, I have," answered she; "but we can all play with them, we can all build, and play at Sally, and you can help to water the plants."

"And all of us shall enjoy their beauty, you know, and the more because our dear little Mary takes care of them," said her mamma. "Now let us call in Susan."

Susan came smiling in from the kitchen, and was immediately

upon by the children, who, after tying a
handkerchief over her eyes, led her up to
a chair, on which lay a dark but bright,
blue merino gown, and a cap trimmed
with cherry-coloured ribbons. When
her eyes were uncovered, and she was
told these were for her, her cheeks
became as red as the ribbons with
pleasure, and she thanked them all in her
prettiest manner. Then they hung over
her arm a green and lilac silk work-bag,
that looked as if it was full of all sorts of
useful things to give to her little assistant
in the kitchen, and then she went away
carrying her presents, for she said she
had not a minute to spare.

James White now ran upstairs, and presently came down again, carrying a large brown paper parcel. They all gathered round him while he untied the string. When he had opened it, there appeared, to the great delight of everybody, a collection of new books; there were a great many children's books, beautifully bound in all manner of colours, red, green, orange, blue, with gilding and pretty ornaments; and most of them had pictures, and they seemed such nice stories. There were larger books too, which were not for the children; he had not forgotten any one. How much pleasure for winter evenings had James

White brought in his brown paper parcel!
They could not help opening the books
and beginning to read, but James White
himself called them away by saying,
" There are still a great many nice things
in this room that we have heard nothing
about; here is a whole box full."

" Oh, you must not touch that box,"
cried Mary, " those are grandmamma's
presents."

" Then is grandmamma to wear this
bright red handkerchief, and this black
velvet cap ?" asked James White.

" Oh, no," answered she, laughing,
"those are for Robin; you know who
ᵀ mean."

"Yes, I know him," said he, "does he still act the Robin?"

"Yes, and we know he will act it at grandmamma's for us, so I hemmed this red handkerchief for his bright red breast, and Chrissy made this black velvet cap for his poll, as he calls it."

"Well, certainly then this warm jacket and trousers and the peaked hat, lying on the chair, *cannot* be for grandmamma," said James White, putting on the hat, which had a scarlet ribbon round it, with a bunch of bright holly-berries at one side.

This made them all laugh so much that it was a long time before any one

could speak; at last Mary said, " Those
are for a little Italian boy we know; he
promised to come here on Christmas
morning, and he is to dine with Susan."

" And has he got a little sister that
is to have these pretty dolls?" said
James White.

" No, he left a little sister at home in
Italy, with his father and mother. He is
all alone here; but he is to go back next
year with all the money he has; then
they will be so happy, he says. The
dolls are for some little girls I know
in the village."

Just then Oliver passed the window
bringing in some logs, and Mary's

mamma called him in and gave him a nicely bound copy of "Robinson Crusoe," with which he was very much pleased, for he was very fond of reading in the evenings.

"And now," said Mary's mamma, "suppose you all go out and leave the dolls and different things at the cottages, like good fairies; but Oliver must take the arm-chairs to Mr. Dove."

"Who is Mr. Dove?" asked James White.

"He is our village carpenter, and you will like him very much."

"And he made the frame-work of these chairs," said Thomas, "and never knew they were for himself and Goody Dove."

"Then mamma had them stuffed," said Mary, "and covered them."

"Is not this a pretty flower worked on the back?" said Willie. "We can take Reuben his trap, bat, and ball."

"Yes, and Jessie her doll," said Mary; "this is hers in the blue frock. But, mamma, we cannot go out yet; we have something more to do."

Just then mamma saw by her side, on a small table which Thomas had wheeled round, a beautiful little ship; it was made of boxwood. It had three masts, and every sail, rope, and yard,

were made correctly. It was covered
by a glass shade, and it stood on a rug
worked in shades of sea-green and white,
to imitate the waves. Thomas took
hold of her hand and asked her with a
beaming face to accept it.

"Oh, it is beautiful," she cried,
"did you really make this for me,
Thomas?"

"We all made it," said he, "mamma
cut out the sails and Willie hemmed
them, and made the flag, and mamma
made the sea that it stands upon, and
gave the glass shade."

"It is a large merchant ship, I see,"
said she; and Mary began to sing a

verse out of her favourite "Oak-tree," by Mary Howitt :—

> " For she shall not be a man-of-war,
> Nor a pirate shall she be,
> But a noble Christian merchant ship,
> To sail upon the sea."

James White said it was famously made, and told Thomas he was a capital workman; and Mary's mamma said that it should stand in the parlour window, and that it would be a pleasure to her whenever she looked at it. Just then she raised her head, and suddenly exclaimed, " Oh, how like! thank you, my dear Chrissy, for such a precious gift. I know it is ˑm you." A curtain had been drawn away that had covered one part of the wall, and there hung a picture of little Mary carrying a basket of flowers on her head. While every one stood looking at it, the little girl herself began to dance and jump about the room, clapping her hands and crying, " That was what we were doing when we shut ourselves in the room ; and papa gave the pretty frame. But you don't know how like it is yet. Come, Chrissy ! come and help me." And away they went together.

In a few minutes they came back, Mary carrying on her head a large flower-basket, exactly like that in the picture. It was made of open wire-work, which

was frosted all over with crystals so as
to look like the trees with their coral
and diamond branches. It was lined
with bright green moss, which looked
lovely with the shining frost-work.
Round the edge of the basket was a
wreath of ivy, and the dark leaves fell
over the edge; within the ivy was a
wreath of winter berries; the bright
holly was most abundant: but there were
also the smooth white snow-berries, the
ivy-berries nearly black, the greenish
white mistletoe, and a few red haws that
the birds thought they might spare.
Next came a gay wreath of flowers, not-
withstanding the early winter, for there

was not a cottage-garden in the village that had not contributed some out of its warm sunny corners, when it was known that little Mary wanted them for her mamma. There were chrysanthemums of every colour, yellow, white, purple, and pink; laurustinus, and china roses. Then came a wreath of geranium leaves, and next to them a wreath of pure wintry-white flowers of the hellebore, which the country people call Christmas roses; these came from Mr. Dove's. Next to them, and in the centre of all, was a splendid bunch of scarlet geranium flowers, that Oliver had been cherishing in his window for a long time.

Little Mary walked straight up to her mamma, holding this beautiful basket on her head with one hand, and said, "Do you like it, dear mamma?"

"I do, indeed, like it, my little darling," said she, kissing the bright face under the basket, which Chrissy removed and held safe, to let the little girl throw her arms round her mamma's neck. "It is a worthy companion to the other beautiful presents I have had to-day."

Every one gathered round this lovely basket, and seemed hardly able to leave off admiring it, till Mary's mamma said, "Put it in the middle of the table, Chrissy."

But the middle of the table was occupied. There stood on it a marble figure of an angel, with large wings folded behind, and hands crossed on the breast. It was a present to Chrissy from all; and as her sweet voice and beaming eyes thanked them, they felt that it was just the right present for her.

"Now let us go and be the good fairies," cried Willie.

"Oh, yes, so we will," said Mary, beginning to collect dolls, balls, frocks, and all manner of things. "Here's something we have forgotten: Bouncer! Bouncer!" A scratching and a short bark were heard at the door, and when

8

it was opened in he came, and received from his master's hands a new brass collar. As soon as it was fastened he gave himself a good shake and made it rattle very much, and then jumped up on Mary, as much as to say, "I am dressed ready to go out;" and they were soon ready·too, and set off, all but Mary's mamma, who wished to stay at home.

When their walk was over, and they had dressed and all met in the little dining-room, they saw why she had not gone out with them. She had made the room look so beautiful! The lovely flower-basket was placed in the middle of the dinner-table; the angel on the

chimney-piece; and the picture of little
Mary beside it. The ship was placed on
one side of the window, and the stand of
flowers on the other; the pretty work-
basket on a table near; also the carrier's
cart, bricks, tool-chest, and Mary's farm.
The books had a little table all to themselves. The setting sun shone in at the
window; the fire blazed, and crackled.
Susan came in to wait in her new gown
and cap; and everything looked as
cheerful as the little party felt. The
parlour was cleared for the evening's
amusements, for after tea there was to
be blind man's buff. They soon found
that James White could romp as well

as talk, and they made such a noise, that at last, to quiet them a little, Mary's mamma sang to them, and sometimes all joined in chorus.

Just as they finished all together, an old Christmas carol that ended with—

"And all the bells in the earth did ring
On Christmas-day in the morning,"—

a merry whistle took up the tune outside the door.

"Robin! Robin! I know it is," cried Mary; and out she rushed followed by every one in the room, and soon returned tight clasped round his neck, while the most joyous welcomes sounded 'rough the room.

Now there was a busy running backwards and forwards of little feet to wait on the newly arrived guest, who had walked twelve miles to come to them, he said, and who brought in some snow on his hat and cloak. He was soon comfortably seated in dry slippers in a warm corner, with a cup of hot coffee and a large slice of cake, which the children took care he should have, and he declared he would have walked *fifty* miles in the snow to be so received, and to find such a set of dear faces all together; and every one felt as if there really was nothing more in the world to wish for.

When tea was over, and Robin had been asked three times if he was *quite* rested, "blind man's buff" began. Who played the most pranks, whether Mary's papa, Robin, or James White, it was difficult to say. Everybody joined, Susan and all, and every one was caught and blinded.   Willie was blind-man three times, and Mary twice. It was very difficult to catch Thomas, for he climbed over places so cleverly, and ran so fast; but he was caught at last. "Puss in the corner" followed, and then "Frog in the middle." When James White was Frog, and they were all dancing round and singing "Frog in the middle and can't get out," he jumped over, but they said that was not fair, that would never do! he must crawl under;" so he had to go in again; but he managed to get through very soon. As for Robin, when he was in the middle, he made such a ridiculous face, so like a frog, that they all lost the strength in their hands with laughing, and he got out directly; Willie was so little he crept under very soon. After this they had " Hunt the ring ;" this is a nice game, not so riotous as " Hunt the slipper." You have a long string, on which you put a ring, and then tie the two ends together; then all but one, who is in the middle, stand in a circle, and push the ring from one to the other, while the one in the middle tries to catch and sto] it, as it is quickly slipped from one to the other. " Magic music " came next. In this game one is sent out of the room while the rest fix on something which that one is to do. Then the music begins. When the one who is trying to find out what had been fixed on, is near doing it, the music is loud; when not nearly finding it out, the music is very low. When Robin was sent out they fixed that, when he came in, he should take up the tongs like a fiddle, and pretend to play a tune on them with the poker. It was a good while before he found out, but he tried so many funny things, while he was about 't, that they were all quite tired with laughing, so they played at "Cross purposes" to rest, and then cried "Forfeits." Then Robin's new black velvet cap and red handkerchief were presented, and he promised to act the Robin in the finest style next day. To finish the merry evening's games they had a dance, while Mary's mamma played to them, and then supper was ready.

What a pleasure it was to the children to sit up to supper! and then all to gather round the fire, while the log blazed, and a pleasant light and warmth seemed to fill the room.

After many a merry joke and laugh had gone round, Mary's papa asked for the Christmas song.   "We can have it again in the morning," said he; "but sing it now, before we part for the night."   So Mary, with the two boys, joined at the end of each verse by her mamma and Chrissy, sang:—

I.

Christmas is come with holly bough,
Red berries peeping through the snow,
That makes the bough droop heavy and low;
And at his beard an icicle
Hangs and shines, while the cold drops trickle.
It is the only thing that's cold,
Upon his face as merry as old.

II.

Christmas is come; see the red fire blazing,
It sends forth sounds with a joy that's amazing;

Glad tidings come with the merry sound
Of the old year's circle rolling round.
Good-bye, Gaffer year, we very well know
You're off on a journey by night through the snow.

III.

Glad tidings we hear! joy, joy, in all faces!
We'll send Time to bed, or to run backward races.
Peace, peace to the world, let the world be all love,
Through Him, the bless'd Teacher, whose light
    beams above.
Young and old—children all—we are sister and
    brother
For His sweet lesson taught us to love one another.

The song seemed to have made every face look happier than even it did before.

"Do you remember, mamma," said Mary, "once, when we were talking about birthdays, you said that Christmas-day was the happiest of all, for it was a birthday for all the world?"

The Curvy Girls
Baby Club

MICHELE GORMAN

Notting Hill Press
PUBLISHING'S THIRD WAY

Please note that this novella is written in British English rather than American English, including all spelling, grammar and punctuation.

Together Again

Chapter 1
JANE

Jane watched Katie do one of those comedy double takes. 'You're… pregnant?!' she said to Ellie, probably louder than she meant to, judging by the startled looks from the people around them. 'I mean, you only moved out a month ago!'

Jane was tempted to point out that there was no scientific link between moving boxes and insemination, but it didn't seem the time. Katie was obviously still smarting about losing her flatmate, though you can't really blame Ellie for wanting to move in with her new husband.

Ellie nodded, the grin spreading across her face. 'I know, isn't it nuts?'

That was one word for it. Jane's head started spinning with the implications of this news. She set

1

down her knitting and climbed out of the pub's booth so she could hug their best friend. 'I think what Katie means is congratulations, sweetheart.'

It might have been her imagination but she swore Ellie was already glowing.

After a few seconds Katie pushed Jane out of the way to launch herself on Ellie. 'I'm so happy for you and Thomas. But please don't ever leave for so long again!'

Ellie giggled, squeezing back. 'You're right, I'm a total cow for going on my honeymoon and I promise not to do it again. I am sorry for not being in touch, though. The internet's so dodgy in the bush and by the time we got to Fiji, well, I had other things on my mind.'

'That's obvious,' Jane said. 'And don't pay any attention to Katie. You and Thomas deserved the month together after all the drama lately.'

'Has he told his mother yet?' Katie asked as they sat again at their usual scarred old pub table in Katie's local. It had been Ellie's local too until she moved in with Thomas on the other side of London.

When Ellie sighed, her peaches and cream complexion reddened. 'It's only been five weeks so we're not telling people yet. We just found out officially a few days ago when the GP confirmed it. It's a honeymoon baby! Thomas is so excited… I'm surprised he's been able to keep it from his mother. She rang nearly every day while we were away, as you'd expect, always with some ridiculous excuse. When she couldn't get through on his mobile she rang the hotel. When she ran out of excuses she said she was checking that he'd put on enough sun cream.'

'That woman needs to get in her box,' Katie said.

True, Jane thought, and then they should post it to the other side of the world for Ellie. Though given that Millicent harassed the honeymooners across a dozen time zones, the distance probably wouldn't matter.

'How on earth will you hold her back once she knows about the baby?' wondered Katie.

'I've no idea but at least I've got two more months before we have to tell her. I made Thomas promise.'

'But he does know you're telling us?' Jane asked, suddenly worried that she was spilling secrets.

Ellie nodded, trying to hold in her smile but completely failing. She did look amazing. She was slightly cheating by wearing white to emphasise her light tan – her pale skin never allowed much more – but even her usually flyaway light brown curls were tamed. Jane could forgive that kind of showing-off (it was only April) when Ellie looked so happy. What a complete turnaround from the days before the wedding.

Her mother-in-law had a lot to answer for.

'When are you due, sweetheart?' Jane asked, feeling herself grinning like a loon.

'You're not going to believe this,' Ellie said. 'Christmas Day! So that's my New Year's Eve ruined. And I'm on orange juice for the rest of the year.' But she didn't look unhappy about being teetotal.

'Better you than me,' said Katie, extracting her purse. 'I'll get the champagne for Jane and me. And a pint of OJ for the mother-to-be.'

'Katie, sweetheart, you'd better sit down for a sec,' Jane said, pulling her gently back into her seat. She'd need a seat when she heard her announcement. 'I'd like to change my order.'

'That's not exactly shocking news, Jane.'

'You'll have to make that two pints of juice.'

'You're not drinking either?' Katie asked. 'When did this start?'

'I guess around the same time as Ellie, as it happens.' She waited for the penny to drop.

Ellie got there first. 'You too?!' she gasped.

'Me too. Can you flippin' believe it? I was going to tell you tonight anyway but then, with your news, I didn't want to steal your thunder just now. It's not as big a deal for me.'

She knew she was lying as she said that.

'Don't be daft, of course it's a big deal,' said Ellie. 'We're having babies together!' Then her mouth fell open. 'And after…'

Jane nodded. After the years she and Andy spent trying for their first child, Matthew, she shouldn't technically even be pregnant without the doctor's help. Although it had to be said that Abigail was conceived the old-fashioned way – after a bottle of wine and a Friday night takeaway – so their reproductive organs did sometimes work.

She rubbed her tummy, which of course wasn't showing yet. The swell beneath her dress was all her.

She caught Katie studying her expression. Of course she knew what she was thinking… what she'd been thinking since she found out. With two children already who hadn't needed nappies in years, not to mention a blooming chat show career, how exactly was this supposed to work? She'd have to stash the baby behind the studio sofa and feed him during the advert breaks.

'Thank you,' Jane said. 'Andy and I are still in shock

but we went to the GP on Tuesday and it is official. We'll be a family of five by the end of the year.' She picked up her knitting again. The clacking needles were always relaxing and just then, she needed to calm down. Another baby!

But Ellie was rightly more concerned about Katie. 'You don't feel left out, do you?' she asked, grabbing her hand.

'Leave me well out of it!' she sputtered. 'I'm absolutely over the moon for both of you, and I can't wait to be an honorary auntie, as long as I don't have to change nappies, but that's enough for me. We're definitely not ready to be parents yet. We've only just moved in together.'

Katie did have a point. It was easy to forget that they hadn't been together forever, but for years Rob was just their fellow Slimming Zone friend, builder of the Curvy Girls Club website and all-round good guy. Then he got to be the love of Katie's life, too. It was a pretty great upgrade.

'But think of the fun you'd have trying to have a baby!' Ellie said, refusing to accept that not everyone wanted morning sickness and stretch marks as the result of a night of passion.

'Urgh, I haven't been able to even think about sex lately,' Katie said.

'Still feeling delicate?' Jane asked. Katie rang her a few days ago between toilet visits to say that her intestines were falling out.

'Much better now, thanks, but please don't ever let me order sushi from a leaflet pushed through the letterbox again… though it has brought up an interesting question, given the circumstances. Let's just say I've had a lot of time to ponder it.'

She narrowed her dark blue eyes at them. 'Should the toilet roll unroll from on top or underneath? Rob and I disagree.'

'On top,' Ellie and Jane said together.

'Thank you. Someone please tell him that, along with everything else he has to learn about being a civilised flatmate. I don't understand why it has to be so hard living with a man. You didn't tell me it would be this hard. I don't mean that in a bad way, but it's a huge adjustment and I loved living with Ellie. We had our routines and we didn't get in each other's way. Now I spend half my time hiding in the loo to take care of the things Rob's not allowed to see… you know… maintenance-wise.'

Ellie nodded. 'Try living in hotel rooms for a month. There's no chance of doing anything private in there. I had to come back to the room during breakfast each day to, ehem, take care of business.'

Jane set her knitting aside. 'Ellie, you're not seriously saying you won't poo with Thomas around? God, Andy and I don't even close the door anymore. Wait a few years. You'll be brushing your teeth while he's on the loo. And trust me; once you've been in the delivery room you won't be shy about the rest of it. Just try keeping the mystery alive after he's seen a person emerge from your vagina.'

'That's charming, Jane, thanks for the image.'

'Do you want to know how big it is?' Ellie asked.

'You're not talking about Jane's…?'

'No, Katie! I mean the baby. Right now it's the size of a hundred-and-thousand. You know, those bits you have on an ice cream.'

'Only one?' Katie asked.

'Believe me,' Jane said. 'You only want one in there.'

Week Five... Mothers

Chapter 2
Ellie

Ellie didn't like dwelling on the past but whenever she thought about her mother-in-law, Millicent, she could feel her blood start to boil. So standing on her doorstep wasn't helping her composure. Nor was the fact that morning sickness seemed to be one of nature's biggest lies. It was nearly 7 p.m. and she felt like vomming in her mother-in-law's hydrangeas.

But she didn't have much choice about being there when Thomas went every Tuesday for dinner. If he knew the depth of her feelings for the woman who gave him life he'd be devastated, so she turned up for the sake of marital harmony, really. The one time she did let her feelings fly, Thomas acted like she'd rubbished Father Christmas.

'Thomas!' Millicent cried when she opened the family's mock-Tudor front door. Millicent was a big believer in keeping Ye Olde England alive, which explained the medieval façade inside London's Zone 4. She'd have dressed Thomas like Oliver Twist if it wouldn't have meant turning him into the school punching bag.

'And Ellie, hello,' she said as an afterthought, coolly appraising her with the same startling green eyes that Thomas had.

Ellie kissed the woman's cheek, holding her breath against her rose-scented perfume. As usual, she was dressed like Princess Margaret about to go walking on the moors, her tartan tweed skirt and worsted hunting jacket looking a bit incongruous over a silk pussy bow blouse. The blouse was black, also as usual, as befitted her status as grieving widow. Never mind that her ex-husband was alive and well and living with his second wife in Surrey.

'Do you have the photos of your holiday?' Millicent wanted to know as they settled on the old-fashioned leather sofas in the sitting room. When Ellie first visited she assumed the house was full of heirlooms. Nobody would choose to have so much brocade, tapestry and tartan if they could help it. But it didn't come from ancestors. It came from online catalogues. Except for the dining table. That belonged to Thomas's dad's family, but it was a sore subject for Millicent so nobody mentioned it.

'I haven't had them printed yet, Mum. I'll try to do it at the weekend.'

'But I've waited over a week to see them!' she cried, jutting her bottom lip out.

Ellie hated when she did that. She knew the beginning of a strop when she saw one. 'I could try to get to Boots to print them out at lunchtime tomorrow,' she offered. Not that her job left her much free time during the day. She tried to recall the meetings scheduled for tomorrow. If she had a mid-morning snack she could hold out for lunch at 3 p.m. after the board meeting.

Thomas grasped her hand. 'No, Ellie, I'm just being selfish. I'll print them out tomorrow, Mum.'

'Oh wonderful, then you can show me at dinner tomorrow night.' She patted her platinum blonde bob. It hardly moved with all the hairspray in there. 'I'll come into town so you don't have to travel.'

Thomas looked confused. How did he not see that coming? 'We have dinner plans tomorrow,' Ellie reminded him.

'I don't want to intrude. I'll come after dinner then,' said Millicent, as if that settled things.

Ellie wouldn't win, so she didn't bother. 'I'll just get some biscuits to go with the cheese,' she said, starting for the kitchen.

'No, dear, this cheese is meant to be eaten on its own. It's French. Have some.'

She was just about to whack off a great slice of brie when she remembered the list of banned foods now that she was eating for two. 'No, thank you. I don't want to spoil my appetite.'

Millicent looked at her as if to say *No chance of that* and all Ellie's insecurities threatened to bob to the surface. She pushed them down again.

And Millicent had wondered why she didn't get invited to go with Ellie and her mum to shop for wedding dresses. It was bad enough for Ellie trying to fit her lumps and bumps into a svelte dream dress. She didn't need Millicent, the Talking Scales, reminding her that she'd been a size eight for thirty years, ever since her own wedding.

It was only a tiny victory, though, keeping her out of

the dress shops, because she'd meddled everywhere else. Ellie had to laugh when she thought about how naïve she'd been when Thomas proposed. She'd imagined their perfect wedding and the fun they'd have planning it together. Her mind raced with ideas about going to see bands they both loved and sampling wedding cakes and choosing a venue.

They did all of that. Only they weren't alone.

When Thomas suggested that Millicent come to the first gig with them, Ellie's heart melted. How close he was to his mother! No wonder he was so sensitive and kind. Of course Millicent could come, she'd told him graciously.

That was before she realised that having a chaperone on their date wouldn't be a one-off.

Her mind was dragged back to the chintzy living room when Millicent asked Thomas about work. As if they hadn't already talked at least once that day. She never asked Ellie about her job, despite the fact that she worked for the same company as Thomas. Perhaps being a secretary wasn't as interesting as being a marketing exec. More likely, she just couldn't give a toss about Ellie's life.

As Thomas described his latest campaign, Ellie glanced at the framed wedding photo on the mahogany table. She looked so happy. And Thomas was gorgeous in his blue tie and light grey morning suit. The only thing marring the photograph was Millicent wedged between them. That pretty much summed up their life together at the moment.

She'd had no idea about any of that at first, though. They'd already been together months before she'd even met Millicent. And she couldn't have been more different than Thomas's description.

Ellie expected a mild-mannered single mum with Thomas's personality – fun, easy-going and kind. Not this blonde-bobbed dragon in tweed.

When they first met, she'd assumed Millicent's lack of questions were out of respect for her privacy. Obviously she was sensitive about prying too much.

Ha! That woman didn't have a sensitive bone in her body, except when it came to herself.

The trouble was, she made her behaviour seem normal and if Ellie objected, somehow it always ended up sounding like she was the one with the problem. Trying wedding cakes? Well, Millicent was an excellent baker and Thomas trusted her palate. Same with the wine and the catering choices. And with her family friends willing to cut a great deal on their wonderful venue, it made sense to go with Millicent's suggestion. Every time Ellie objected there seemed to be a perfectly good reason to let Thomas's mother get her way.

Until the day that an unstoppable force met an immovable object.

'You're not inviting *that woman* to the wedding?' she'd asked as she scanned the excel sheet that Thomas had printed out for her.

They both knew who she meant. There'd been a lot of discussion about that woman. 'Mum, please. She's married to Dad. She has to come.'

'And I suppose you expect me to sit next to her in the church? At the dinner? Oh Thomas, how could you?'

Tears brimmed in Millicent's eyes. For once even Ellie felt sorry for her. It couldn't have been easy when

Millicent split up with Thomas's dad, Jack. It wasn't one of those blameless divorces where friends got to stay neutral. Jack fell in love with his work colleague, Suki, and everybody except Millicent knew it. The process of unwinding their marriage was as humiliating for her as it was painful.

'She's Dad's wife, Mum. I can't not invite her.'

'It's your wedding. You can do what you want.'

Ellie nearly snorted at that. As if.

'Dad won't come unless she's invited.'

'What a terrible situation for him to put you in. It's just selfish,' she said without any trace of irony.

The look of anguish on Thomas's face made Ellie want to protect him. 'Millicent, please be reasonable. We can seat you away from them. You won't even have to speak.'

'So now I'm to be banished at my only son's wedding? Thank you very much, but no, dear, that's not acceptable.'

There was no trace of tears now, Ellie noted. 'I didn't mean you'd be banished. We can seat *them* away from you. You're the mother of the groom. That makes you the second most important person there.'

Millicent allowed herself a tiny smile. 'Well, since Thomas is most important, I suppose I'll have to live with her being there.'

Just a minute, thought Ellie. That makes me third? 'That's not—' But she didn't finish. The important thing was that both of Thomas's parents would be there on his wedding day.

Having sniffed victory, though, Millicent seemed to have a new demand every day in the run-up to the wedding... 'Seat them on the bride's side,' she'd said.

'They can sit in the row behind you,' Thomas proposed.

'Don't let them walk down the aisle with me.'

'You'll be walking down the aisle with me, Mum. Ellie's dad will walk her down and you can walk me down. Dad will walk in with the regular guests.'

'I want to make the toast to you.'

'Of course. And then Dad might want to say something after you.'

'Tell that bitch not to wear teal. That's my colour.'

'We'll send an email out to everyone telling them not to wear your colour or Ellie's mum's.'

And so it went on, negotiations sometimes getting more delicate than the Palestine-Israel conflict. Ellie had to hand it to Thomas. He'd do well in the diplomatic services.

One thing was for sure. She'd never be that kind of smother mother.

She grinned. She was going to be a mother! They just had to keep Millicent from finding out for a few more months.

Week Seven… Congratulations, it's a Revel

Chapter 3
JANE

Jane stood in her kitchen with a spoon in one hand and a damp trainer in the other, trying to remember what she was supposed to be doing. The pregnancy brain couldn't have kicked in yet – she was still in the enormous boob phase.

'Mum!' her daughter said. 'We're going to be late. May I have my spoon, please?'

Right. It was her turn to feed the children so Andy could take them to school. She set the whiffy trainer on the worktop to get Matthew's cereal.

'That's not very hygienic,' he protested. 'We could get toxocariasis.'

'You're not going to get toxi-anything, now eat your cereal,' she said, stuffing the shoes into his rucksack.

'I don't want toxocariasis!' Abby said through a mouth full of porridge.

'Well, you're in luck, because there's none going. Do you need your gym kit today?'

Abby shook her head. 'Just three tins for the food bank donation.'

'Why didn't you tell me that yesterday when we went to Aldi after school?'

'I forgot.'

Jane sank to her knees to peer into the bottom shelf of the mostly-empty pantry. It wasn't promising. There was a tinned steak and kidney pudding. Where had that even come from? She put it back. Nobody wants to be known as the family who eats tinned meat pies. There were a few tins of lentils that she'd optimistically bought months ago, half a dozen tins of tuna and a box of macaroni and cheese that was Andy's guilty pleasure.

Andy came into the kitchen just as she was getting to her feet.

'Sweetheart, can I donate your macaroni and cheese for the food bank please?'

He smiled and kissed her. 'It's for a good cause.'

'Yes, those poor children probably don't get enough orange food colouring.'

'Mum, can I have mac and cheese?' asked Matthew.

'Absolutely not.'

'But you let Dad have it.'

'You can't have it because it'll stunt your growth. Your father would have been three inches taller if it hadn't been for the mac and cheese.' She turned back to Andy. 'I'll be home by two to pick up the children.'

'I'll get something for dinner. Any preferences? Or cravings?'

'No, not yet. Just get some chicken from Nando's. We've got stuff for salad. I've got to dry my hair. You're okay here?'

'Yep, see you later.' He bent down to gently kiss Jane's tummy, making the children wretch with disgust.

He laughed, reaching for Abby before she could

escape from her chair. He blew a particularly wet raspberry on her skinny little tummy, sending her into fits of giggles.

Jane loved watching her family when they were all together like that. Abby and Matthew were terrific children, demands aside, but it hadn't been easy when they were babies. And now they were about to do it all again. She felt tired just thinking about it.

Andy would share the sleepless nights and nappy changes, she knew, just like he'd done with Matthew and Abby. She just didn't want either of them to have to go through it again. And, being selfish, especially now that she was building her career again.

She got to the studio and into the makeup chair a bit before nine, nice and early. The make-up artist swept her hair off her face with a clip and got to work sponging on the foundation that would keep the harsh lights from washing out her complexion. She always liked the way they did her eyes, heavy with liner and shadow, though she never seemed to have the time for more than a slick of lip gloss and maybe some mascara on non-telly days.

By the time the stylist finished straightening and smoothing her hair, it swung thick, blonde and shiny from her shoulders. No wonder she always tried to plan social meetings on programme days.

Jane thought of this preparation as putting on her game-face. The make-up did its best to make her camera-ready, and the time before the show made sure she didn't implode with nerves on air.

Considering that their viewership would fit inside Wembley Stadium without anyone having to sit next to another person, she really shouldn't have been so nervous. And as soon as the cameras started rolling, usually she wasn't. But till that second there were always those few moments when she wished for her old behind-the-camera producing job back.

She'd nearly finished the pre-show routine when Kirk sat carefully in the chair beside her with Kleenex already stuffed into his shirt collar. 'Nice weekend?' he asked as the make-up artist got to work on him.

Jane never did see what was supposed to be so appealing about her co-host. When he agreed to join the show the producers acted like they'd bagged Bradley Cooper, not a fifty-five-year-old actor who was on *Coronation Street* in the eighties. He still had most of his hair, light brown and wavy, and wore it a bit long at the front to disguise the plugs. They didn't show up on-screen but she could never look at his hairline without thinking of Abby's Barbie.

He did have quite striking blue eyes and he laughed a lot, which was charming. All in all he wasn't a bad person to spend an hour with twice a week, but supposedly their audience wet their knickers over him.

'Yes, good thanks,' Jane said. 'Did you do anything nice?' She didn't feel like talking. Having asked him about himself, now she wouldn't have to.

'There's a new club on the King's Road. Blasé, have you been?' He didn't wait for an answer. He never did. 'We should go sometime. You'd love it.'

She smiled patiently. Kirk didn't read his audience any better when they were on air. She could just imagine what the twenty-two-year-old Blasé clientele, in their micro-dresses and stilettos, would make of her. 'Mmm, that would be fun,' she said, knowing full well he'd never mention it again. He was just limbering up for their show.

They were practically contractually obliged to flirt on-air. When Jane first talked to the producers she wasn't sure about that. Hell, she wasn't even certain she wanted to go back into presenting but, after all the therapy, at least she could contemplate it. And Andy was wholeheartedly behind her, flirting and all, so she went for it.

Just as she went to turn off her phone, a text came through.

Seven weeks. Our babies are the size of a Revel. Ellie xx
            Which one? She typed back quickly.
Coffee. Xx

            Euch. xo

She turned her phone off as the thought of coffee sent a queasy wave through her.

Kirk winked as usual just as the intro music began and the audience lights dimmed. Their set was designed as a cosy front room. They sat in stripy upholstered armchairs with silk-fringed reading lamps over their shoulders. It was just like being in Jane's front room, except for the live studio audience, nicer furniture, lack of school books, PlayStations, piles of clean laundry waiting to be folded, and empty mugs that her family seemed genetically programmed to ignore.

'Let's get happy, London!' Kirk said. 'And hello, Jane, you're looking gorgeous as usual.'

She glanced at her pale green day dress, one of about a dozen that she wore on camera. Like everything else about the show, her style was viewer-approved. 'Thanks Kirk, it must be the new shower gel I used this morning,' she answered as per the script they'd worked up while in the make-up chairs.

'Lucky shower gel,' he murmured to the delight of the studio audience, and the show carried on as usual.

Thanks to their shoestring budget it was rare that they had real live guests, so Jane was looking forward to the morning. They were no Paxman and Parky in their questioning but it did give them something to talk about other than the best holiday beaches and who wore what on the red carpet.

Not that they didn't still have to cover the basics. 'Are you looking forward to your holiday?' she asked. He was due to spend two weeks chasing twenty-something backpackers on India's west coast and Jane couldn't wait to host the show on her own.

'My sun cream and swim trunks are packed,' he said.

Jane tried not to imagine Kirk in swim trunks. Or applying sun cream.

'It sounds like bliss.' She gave the camera a meaningful look.

He grasped her hand. 'Come with me. We'll run away together.'

The audience cheered.

'But someone has to stay to do the show.' She tried to look devastated at the sacrifice she was making.

Their show was like working for the World Wrestling Federation, without the muscles or leaps from the top rope. The fans suspended disbelief that lust could bloom between a thirty-four-year-old chubby mother-of-two and a has-been actor twenty years her senior. Everyone knew Kirk and Jane were pretending but it didn't keep them from loving it. 'And speaking of the show,' she said. 'We've got a wonderful treat today. Tracy Chaplin never dreamed she'd turn her love of baking into her full-time job, but after winning *Britain's Got Baking Talent*, her life has changed. Please welcome Tracy!'

The demure-looking forty-something woman hurried on set.

'We're really glad to have you on the show, Tracy,' said Kirk. 'And personally I can't tell you how happy I am to hear more about your leavening agents.'

Oh no, not even thirty seconds had passed. Jane rushed to add, 'Yes, we all love a good rise! I saw some of your cakes and they were amazing. But how did it all start, Tracy? Because this was the first baking competition you've ever entered, right?'

'Nice one, Jane,' said one of their producers, Harriet, into her earpiece. Though it wasn't a live show, she liked to keep the cameras rolling if possible. Unbeknownst to Kirk, Jane was under strict instructions to head off any of his innuendos about iced buns or soggy bottoms that might send their guest storming off-set.

'I've always loved baking for my family and friends,' Tracy was saying. 'And I've got a sweet tooth myself.'

'You and me both,' Jane said, patting her tummy. Her love of good food was a bit of a trademark on the show. When the producers ran their focus groups they found that the audience wanted to live vicariously through someone like Jane, and that meant imagining all of the second-hand pleasure with none of the guilt. Loving cakes was one thing. Admitting to weight issues was a strict no-no.

Sometimes she marvelled at how far she'd come on that point. There was a time when she'd have tried any nutty diet to shed some pounds. Funny how a near-death experience and a lot of therapy could change all that.

But it was really thanks to Katie and Ellie and the Curvy Girls Club. And to Pixie too, their fourth founding member, even though they didn't talk much now that she was living in Manchester. Their mantra was all about being happy in their skin. Not that it was always easy to remember when she looked in the mirror, but at least she tried.

'Your family must be so pleased that you've won!' Kirk said. 'They've got a real live celebrity in the family now.'

Tracy blushed through the thick make-up. 'They've never really bothered much with me,' she murmured. 'To tell the truth, sometimes they don't even notice I'm there.'

Jane's heart lurched. 'Well, I'm sure that's not true.'

'Oh, but it is,' said Tracy. 'My husband tells me all the time what a waste of space I am. So it was nice to win something.'

'Lighten up, lighten up!' Harriet was screaming in Jane's ear piece.

What she wanted to do was hug the poor woman, but the show must go on. 'I bet it was wonderful to take part in the competition, doing what you love. Tell us about your winning bake. It must have been tremendous!'

Kirk jumped in to add 'And what we all want to know is, did you lick the bowl?'

'Mayday, mayday, we're going down!' Harriet joked.

'Everybody licks the bowl. Don't we?' Jane asked the audience.

They cheered and another sexual harassment bullet passed safely by.

Harriet gave her a thumbs up from off-camera.

All in a day's work, Jane thought.

Week 8… Lightning Strikes

Chapter 4
Ellie

Ellie had that Friday feeling and couldn't wait to see her friends… especially since these nights would probably get rarer as due dates closed in. It was only a month since she and Thomas found out about the baby and already there were things she couldn't do. So far they mostly involved activities that made her wretch like opening tins of tuna, sardines or any other smelly food, taking out the rubbish or getting within ten feet of kitchen spray, which stank like rotting fruit. She was sure that list would expand along with her tummy.

She spotted Katie's shiny black hair rising up the Tube's escalator. Jane was right behind her. 'All right?' she said as they all kissed hello.

'This is exciting!' said Jane. 'We never go out round here. That makes us hipsters!' She glanced at her thighs. 'Hip-sters, get it?'

'It wasn't exactly an obscure reference,' Katie replied. 'I've got directions. It's the opposite way from the office.'

When they first started the Curvy Girls Club, Rob

found some space in his cousin's workshop just around the corner from the Tube station. It wasn't exactly Knightsbridge, Ellie thought as a man and a woman staggered towards them. They were skinny and vacant-eyed, clutching cans of lager.

She pulled her handbag closer. 'It never feels any safer around here, does it?'

Katie shrugged. 'You're the one who wanted the authentic experience. I suggested jazz bingo in Soho, remember?'

Ellie glanced again at the skinny couple. 'Do you think they're junkies?'

'I think they put the heroin in heroin chic,' whispered Jane just as the woman started screaming at the man about stealing money from her bra.

They quickly followed Katie's directions to the bingo.

The imposing white-fronted building looked like it might once have been a cinema. They didn't exactly blend into the boisterous crowd standing outside puffing on cigarettes. No trendy vapes for them. This was old school.

'Did we take the Tube to the nineteen seventies?' Katie murmured.

'No, I think we're in Albert Square,' whispered Jane.

Ellie started humming the *EastEnders* theme tune.

Most of the clientele were old enough to collect pensions and didn't look like they'd spent much pampering time at the spa. A few glanced their way but nobody seemed very interested in them. Ellie was glad for that.

Inside was filled with booths upholstered in bright purple and red geometric patterns, like an American diner on steroids. Orange and pink walls and flocked carpet shouted over the seating. Nobody would ever accuse the decorators of understatement.

Once they found one of the few empty tables they dared to look around at the competition. They were mostly women, and some had arranged plush toys and other colourful items on their table. Good luck charms. Ellie wished she'd brought something.

'Don't say I don't show you a good time!' Katie said. 'Though I don't think this would work for a Curvy Girls Club's event.'

As the only one of them who worked full time for the Curvy Girls Club, Katie was always on the lookout for activities to offer their members.

'No, the regulars here won't welcome too many of us outsiders crashing their bingo night,' Ellie said. 'But I'm glad we've come!'

Within a few minutes the man on stage with the microphone started calling out numbers. At which point Ellie and her friends failed at bingo.

'What number was that?' Jane asked.

'Sixteen.'

'Hang on. Oh, I've got that one!' She looked very pleased with herself.

'I can't keep track of my tickets,' said Ellie. 'What was the number before the last one?'

'Thirty-seven… or thirty-two,' Jane said. 'How are you finding your numbers so fast, Katie? I can't keep track of them.'

'Ssh! I'm trying to concentrate,' Katie snapped. Ellie hadn't seen her so stressed since her cold-calling days.

'I've had enough,' she said when they finally got to the break. 'We'll never win anything at this rate. I've missed half the numbers. Let's go to the pub. We're really only here to gossip anyway, right?'

Just along the pavement they found a sign pointing down a short alley to the Sebright Arms. A wall of heat and noise hit them as they pushed through the pub doors.

It was much more their speed. Ornate wood panelling lined the walls and bar and the banquets were covered in the requisite red velvet, worn shiny by drinkers' arses. Though full, there was a free corner at one of the long tables. 'I'll get drinks,' Katie said. 'The rounds are cheap now that you two are up the duff.' She went to the bar and ordered herself a large glass of red.

'Thinking about your baby?' Katie asked when she got back, seeing Ellie patting her tummy.

She grinned. 'I can't stop thinking about him.'

'Him? You think it's a boy? Do you think he'll look like Thomas?' She set their lime-and-sodas on the table and took a sip of her wine.

'Maybe,' Ellie said. 'I'd love that.' She considered Katie. 'When you have babies I hope they look like you. Imagine. She'd look like a china doll with your dark hair and pale skin and blue eyes. Maybe she could have Rob's, I don't know, his smile. You must have looked like an Irish girl when you were little.'

Katie laughed. 'I haven't got an Irish bone in my body so I don't know where these looks came from. And no, I was an ugly child. Even my mum admitted it. So hopefully any babies we have will look like Rob, at least when they're small. But that's way off. Till then I'm living vicariously through you two.'

Ellie smiled. 'At least wait till the morning sickness

is over before you live through me.'

'And the sore boobs,' Jane added. 'You're getting sick, Ellie?'

'Oh god, yes,' she said. 'Morning, noon and night. You?'

'It's not too bad. For me it's mostly the boob thing and the exhaustion.'

'I left work early today,' Ellie said. 'I had to have a nap before coming out. Jane, please tell me it gets better.'

She nodded. 'It does, but probably not before it gets worse. Sorry.'

Ellie's mobile rang on Saturday morning just as she was stabbing holes in the lamb shoulder where, the recipe claimed, rosemary had to be stuffed. No wonder sensible people bought their entrees from M&S. She'd have to call Katie back when she'd finished mutilating lunch.

The mobile stopped and almost immediately her landline started ringing. Katie wasn't giving up.

Ellie left a fatty fingerprint on the phone as she answered it. 'Hi, I'm just in the middle of making lunch before Thomas gets back from football. I'm trying roast lamb, from scratch, can you believe it?!'

'I'm pregnant,' said Katie. 'Can you believe that?'

Ellie set the knife down. Then she sat down. 'How are you pregnant?'

'What do you mean *how*, Ellie? How do you think!'

'But you're on the pill. Did you forget to take it?'

'I definitely didn't forget to take it,' said Katie, sounding weary. 'You know how obsessive I am about it.'

'I know. That's why I asked. How do you feel?' Ellie's grin spread over her face. Katie was pregnant too!

'Sick.'

'Morning sickness?'

'Not just that.'

Her grin faltered. 'Are you upset?'

'Well, I'm not happy.'

'You've told Rob, right?'

'He's sitting on the sofa staring at me. I think he's in shock. Yes, he's nodding. He's in shock. That makes two of us. We're supposed to drink brandy or something, right? Except that now I can't. Oh god, I had wine last night. I've probably pickled the baby.'

'No I'm sure you haven't!' said Ellie, not sure whether that was true. 'How pregnant are you anyway?'

'All the way pregnant, I'd say.'

'I mean how many weeks?'

'I'm not sure. You know my periods are all over the place. I felt terrible when I woke up this morning but I assumed it was a hangover, or maybe another bout of food poisoning. But my boobs are killing me even though I've not got my period. And then I remembered what you two were saying last night about the sickness and the boobs and the exhaustion and I thought, no way. I'm on the pill. I can't be. But just to make sure I weed on the stick. Maybe I pooed out the pill when I was ill. Or threw it up. I guess I'll have to go to the GP to find out for sure but Ellie, I'm scared.'

Ellie glanced at the worktop full of ingredients for the roast. Sod the lamb. This was more important. 'Do you want to come over?'

'No, thanks. Rob's here and I guess we should work

it out ourselves. I'll give Jane a ring now. It'll be all right, won't it? Lie to me and tell me it'll be all right.'

'Of course it will and I'm not even lying! This is a wonderful thing, Katie. You and Rob love each other and now you're going to have a baby together.'

'Oh god, I think I'm going to be sick.'

The call ended.

With anyone else, Ellie would have put her shoes on and pocketed her house keys before she'd hung up. But Katie had Rob and there wasn't a better person to keep her calm. Once the shock wore off they'd be fine. Rob was always sensible, kind and reliable. Now he was going to make a fantastic father.

And of course Katie would be a great mum, too, once she got used to the idea.

The doorbell rang just as Ellie finished peeling the potatoes for the roasties without lopping off any of her fingers.

Katie must have changed her mind about coming over!

She grabbed a tea towel to wipe her hands and hurried to the front door. 'I thought you might need a hug!' she said as she flung the door open.

Millicent didn't look like she needed a hug. 'I beg your pardon?'

'Oh! I thought you were someone else.' Self-consciously she adjusted her jogging bottoms and pulled at the tee shirt that she'd slept in last night. As if her mother-in-law didn't make her feel frumpy enough.

'Is Thomas at home?' She peered over Ellie's shoulder.

'No, sorry,' she said, not moving to let her in. 'He's playing football. He won't be back for half an hour.'

She resisted the urge to shoo the woman away from the door.

'That's all right, I don't mind waiting.'

'Well, actually, I'm just cooking lunch.' And the last thing she wanted was for Michelin-Star-Millicent looking over her shoulder while she tried to cook something edible.

'I'd love to, thank you!' said Millicent. 'And of course I don't mind helping you cook.' She pushed past Ellie towards the kitchen, depositing her raincoat on the sofa in the process. It was a rare spot of colour, if khaki could be called a colour, in her otherwise-black ensemble. Morticia Addams does countryside.

'Oh, I'm not a big fan of lamb, dear,' she said when she spotted Ellie's lunch attempt. 'It's too fatty. That's not really good for you, you know.'

She was acting like she'd been invited. Ellie struggled not to raise her voice. 'Well, you know what they say. Everything in moderation is okay.'

'Thomas doesn't eat much of it, does he? He was always very trim and healthy.'

The past-tense implication was clear. 'We don't have it often. It's a treat. Don't feel you have to eat it.'

Or stay.

'No dear, don't worry about me, I can always fix something healthy for myself.' When she glanced around the kitchen, Ellie felt like the dirty dishes in the sink were multiplying before their eyes. And she'd meant to sweep the floor.

'Is Colleen coming back for lunch?' Millicent asked.

'No, why would she?' Ellie felt herself redden. Colleen was Thomas's friend. She was also their co-worker and, on Saturdays, Thomas's footie team's wingback. Try as she might – and she did try for Thomas's sake –Ellie just couldn't make herself like the woman. 'Did Thomas say he was bringing Colleen back?'

'I haven't talked to him this morning. His phone has been turned off.'

Ellie hid her smile. They'd agreed to keep their phones off on weekend mornings. Thomas thought it was so Ellie could avoid talking to her mum, but it wasn't her mum she wanted to avoid.

'I just assumed they'd have lunch together after their match,' Millicent continued, innocent as you please, and Ellie knew what was coming next.

'They've always been so close. He used to bring her home for school holidays, you know.'

Yes, Ellie knew very well. Her mother-in-law was nothing if not predictable and this was her favourite One-Who-Got-Away story.

'Oh, we did have fun together!' she continued. 'She's such a lovely girl, don't you think? She's always been very welcome in our house.'

'As I imagine any of Thomas's friends would be.' She stabbed at the lamb.

'Of course, but Colleen is special.' Millicent giggled. 'We always assumed there was more to their relationship than Thomas let on.'

Stab stab stab. It was easy to be perfect in small doses, she thought, when you're visiting someone for the weekend. Of course you're on your best behaviour. Just try being perfect (or even good enough) when you're in the real world trying to make a life for yourself and your husband with someone breathing down your neck every second of every day, second-guessing and contradicting and doing everything possible to make you feel like you're a poor choice for her son and he'd have been better off marrying his great friend Colleen. Just try being perfect then.

'Dear, I think the lamb is tender enough now.'

Ellie looked down. Their lunch looked like it had been hit by a shotgun blast. 'Yes, thank you, it's just the way I want it.' She shoved it into the oven. 'I'll just peel the carrots. Are you sure this isn't boring for you?'

'No, dear, Thomas will be home soon.' She moved around the kitchen opening cabinets. She adjusted something in every one. A dish to the left, a cup to the right, a little pot of cocktail sticks to the shelf above.

'We're not really settled in yet.' Ellie felt the need to defend her cabinets. 'We're out of the boxes but I haven't organised anything.'

'It takes time,' said Millicent. 'When Thomas's father and I were first married I took ages to set up house. I wanted everything to be perfect.'

Ellie never knew whether to ignore these reflections or encourage them. Millicent could be volatile on the subject of her ex-husband. On the other hand, she often talked about him with such affection that Ellie hated to deprive her of the chance.

'Where was your first house together?'

Millicent made a little snort of surprise. 'Well, you've been there plenty of times, dear.'

'I didn't realise that was your original house. That's a long time to be in one place.'

'Of course it's been redecorated, but it will be thirty years in July. Since I was married.'

Ellie wasn't sure that keeping track of your wedding anniversary nearly a decade after your divorce was altogether healthy. 'We won't stay in this flat that long,' she said. 'We'd like to buy something, maybe next year.'

The flat was nice, on the ground floor with a little garden, but they'd have to find something bigger unless they wanted the baby to sleep in the chest of drawers. Not that she'd breathe a word of that until she had to.

Millicent perked up. 'Someone's at the door. Is it Thomas?' She rushed from the kitchen to welcome her son home.

Ellie slumped against the worktop. God she needed a nap. But there was no way Millicent would leave now.

She grabbed her mobile and sent a quick text to Jane. *Week 8: The babies are the size of a skittle Ellie xx*

Something that small shouldn't be taking so much energy, she thought as she went to welcome Thomas home.

Week Eleven… Where's the Fun in Fun-size Sweets?

Chapter 5
JANE

Jane knew she shouldn't be grumpy about having Kirk back on the show when he had every right to be there. It was just that after two weeks in a sexual innuendo-free zone, it was hard to look convincingly pleased at his return.

But she was a professional, so instead of flouncing off in a huff that her eight-year-old would admire, Jane made small talk when he arrived for make-up.

Starting with what he'd done to his face.

'You look… refreshed,' she said as they settled into their make-up chairs. His skin was the colour of her mother's dining table, and just as shiny.

Kirk stroked his bushy new beard, which didn't suffer from the same follicle challenges as his scalp had. 'Goa was totally awesome, man. You have to see it.'

He practically made the surfer's *hang ten dude* hand signal, embarrassing for a fifty-something man. Jane hoped he wasn't going to speak in 1980s teenage vernacular on the show. 'And you're growing your beard?'

'I was told it makes me look younger.'

It did, though Jane was partial to clean-shaven men. Andy was nearly hairless from his forehead down. She wished she could say the same – lately she'd grown enough chin stubble for them both.

'What do you think?' Kirk said to his make-up artist. 'Does the beard suit me?'

'Definitely,' she said, blotting away his sheen with her powder sponge. 'I like beards. My dad's had one for years.'

His face froze for a second but he chose to forgive the parallel being drawn. 'No live guests today?' he asked Jane, scanning the running order. 'We really should have more. We're getting killed by the likes of *Good Morning London* and *On The Couch*.'

'Psh, Kirk, I love your optimism, but be realistic. We get beaten by the McCain's Oven Chips adverts. We're not exactly in the same league as *On The Couch*.'

It wasn't like their lack of live guests was solely to blame anyway.

The trouble with moving from one side of a business to the other was that it required a total change of perspective. When Jane was producing shows she concerned herself with all the same things her producers now did. Ratings and ratings and, well, ratings. Now on set, she worried instead whether she was getting the good lines and if the camera really did add only twenty pounds.

And yet she couldn't completely ignore her old producer's instinct. She'd make changes if it were her show to run. Emotions would be allowed and they might even (gasp, horror) sometimes talk about real issues.

Not that she ever said any of that out loud. She wasn't naïve. With a name like *Get Happy London*, they weren't exactly competing with *Newsnight*. Their producers liked Jane as a co-host. They wouldn't like her opinions on how they did their jobs.

'I'll talk to the producers about getting more guests on,' Kirk said grandly, like he'd offered to talk to his great mate, Stephen Spielberg.

Sometimes she felt bad for him. At one point in his career he could have said something like that without sounding like a completely delusional twit.

But they shared coffee-fetching duties with their producers, so they had to face the facts. This was regional television. They were hardly in line to be BAFTA-nominated.

'Five, four, three, two, one,' Harriet counted down. The cameras began to roll.

'Let's get happy London!' Jane said, smiling for the camera. 'And look who's back!'

The studio audience cheered. Like a lot of programmes they gave out free tickets to draw in enthusiastic crowds. They didn't have rules about how often one could apply and Jane was pretty sure a number of hard-core fans came to every show.

'Did you miss me?' Kirk asked, unable to resist fishing for the extra dose of adoration.

'We did! And I bet you missed London, too, while you were lying on that beautiful beach eating tropical fruit. We've had the coldest June for twenty years. And the rain's been an extra treat, hasn't it? But you're back now, our little ray of sunshine.'

They took a moment to share a look that sent the audience into a chorus of ahhs, and the rest of the show galloped along at an easy pace. Hard-hitting topics were analysed at length, from Cheryl Cole's new haircut and the high pollen count in the city, to Simon Pegg's upcoming film and whether open-toed boots were the footwear for summer.

Sometimes Jane felt like she could do it in her sleep.

She couldn't get comfortable on the Tube ride from the studio. Her back ached but that wasn't the real problem. It was the seat. Or more specifically, its lack of arm rest. No matter how she sat, her thigh was pushed up against the woman next to her, who was no runway model herself. At some point between South Ken and Sloane Square a look passed between them. I'm sorry I'm making you uncomfortable but I can't help it. Jane bit down her embarrassment, noting how few men ever bothered with this consideration over personal space. She counted six male undercarriages clearly visible thanks to the splayed legs all around her.

As they passed above ground her phone dinged.

Our babies are the size of a fun size Bounty! Ellie xx
Where's the fun in that? J xo

By the time Jane got to the children's school her fat feelings had nearly subsided but she was getting them more often lately. That frightened her more than anything.

Abby ran towards her. 'Mummy!' When she stopped her backpack nearly pulled her backwards. She was the scholar in the family, always toting twice as many books as she needed to.

She threw herself into Jane's waiting arms.

'Hello, Matthew,' she said, nodding cordially to her son and nearly managing to hide her smile as he sidled up beside Abby. They'd agreed this greeting after he confessed that one of his classmates had teased him till he cried for daring to call Jane Mummy in public.

'All right?' he said.

'Did you have a good day?'

'Yes thank you, Mu—' He caught himself just in time and Jane's heart broke a little.

She'd have given anything for them not to face peer pressure yet. They were only babies. At least she was a grown-up by the time it happened to her.

Knowing those thoughts would only spiral downwards, she said, 'I have an idea. Shall we go to the zoo?'

'As long as we don't get toxocariasis,' Matthew said.

'Still on toxocariasis alert, are we? Just don't put a big warm steamy pile of dog poo in your mouth and you won't have to worry about it.' Jane took a moment to savour the look of disgust on her son's face. It wasn't often she got to out-gross him. 'We'll see if Daddy can bunk off from work and come with us.'

She was pretty sure Andy would join them. He claimed to always be busy at work but she could usually get him to come out. His flexible work ethic was one of the (many) things she loved about him.

'Hi, sweetheart, are you busy?' Jane said into the mobile. She knew he'd say yes without giving any detail. That was out of courtesy rather than secrecy, because Jane had a mental block the size of the polar ice cap when it came to Andy's job. He said IT programming was no harder than learning a language but she'd never been able to do that either. As long as their computer at home let her occasionally shop on eBay she was fine not knowing why.

'I'm about to proposition you,' she said.

'I like the sound of that.' She could hear him smiling.

'Meet us at the zoo in half an hour. I just want to pick up a snack for the children first. And something for myself.' There seemed to be no bottom to the pit of Jane's stomach lately.

That was a problem. Every day she could feel the lid on her insecurities loosening a bit. Even after working so hard to get where she was, in a headspace that didn't focus on her size, she was still just one slip of the scales away from ruining everything again.

Her façade as a well-adjusted thirty-something woman didn't stay standing without a lot of shoring up. Katie sometimes asked her whether she could even imagine going back to her wicked old ways. Every day, Jane wanted to tell her. But she always said no, because after nearly a year of therapy to break her extreme dieting habit, one doesn't like to remind loved ones how easily it could all happen again.

Not that she'd jump head first back into diet pills (especially not after promising Andy) but seeing her body change with the pregnancy was leading her on to dangerous ground.

'I feel like you're getting me there under false pretences,' Andy teased, thankfully pulling her away from that steep edge. 'No monkeying around in the monkey house?'

'That's what got me into this condition in the first

place. I'll see you in half an hour.'

Week Thirteen… Who Wants Chinese?

Chapter 6
ELLIE

Something about being pregnant was making Ellie think she was Nigella Lawson without the eyeliner. Not that she could cook for toffee but, generally to Thomas's dismay, she was determined to try. Quite why she thought she'd start with cheese soufflé, she had no idea.

Separating the egg yolks from the whites was beyond her but she did scoop most of the yellow out of the white, and as it all went into the recipe at some point anyway, it shouldn't matter too much.

While the milk was heating up she texted Katie. Now that she'd had nearly two months to get used to the idea of being pregnant, she didn't feel quite so aggrieved. As long as it didn't interfere with the Curvy Girls Club, because that was Katie's real baby.

Ellie bought her *What To Expect When You're Expecting* but hadn't dared broach the idea of antenatal classes yet. Baby steps.

Ellie smiled at her own joke as she texted.

Right now your baby is the size of a Malteser. Isn't that amazing? Ellie xx

She waited for a reply.
Nothing. Then…

Sorry, that Malteser just had my head in the toilet. Katie x

Oh no! Can you eat a piece of toast or something?

That's what I just sicked up. How much longer?

You should feel better in a few weeks. Ellie xx

I don't believe you. K

Then she texted Jane.

The babies are the size of an egg roll! Ellie xx

Ooh I could murder a Chinese, xo came Jane's reply.

A hissing sound caught her attention as she put away her phone. 'Oh shit!' The milk was angrily frothing over the sides of the little pot. It calmed down when she snatched it from the heat, but left a scalded milk ring on the electric hob. She poured in a little more milk from the fridge to make up for any loss and got to work stirring the flour into the butter.
'How the hell is that supposed to work?' she muttered, blowing a curly lock out of her eyes. The butter just swirled around and around in the flour, sending little white poufs across the kitchen every time

she tried to get some leverage with the wooden spoon.

Giving up, she tipped it into the milk and watched the whole mixture seize up like drying cement.

She jumped when she heard someone behind her. 'What are you doing?' Thomas asked, wrapping his arms around her waist as she stared into the pot.

'I was trying to make cheese soufflés. I didn't hear you come in.'

He craned his neck over her shoulder. 'Is it supposed to look like that?'

'Definitely not. We can order takeaway.'

He turned her round so that his face was a few inches from hers. 'Thank you for trying. I'm sure it would have been delicious.'

She laughed. 'It wasn't even edible, but I appreciate the vote of confidence. How was the match?'

He kissed her nose and moved to the kitchen chair to take off his trainers. 'I really don't like playing so late in the day. Mornings are better. We lost, but it was close. I nearly scored. Colleen did score one.'

'Oh, good. I bet she was happy.' It wasn't usually too hard to feign affection for her husband's friend, as long as she didn't have to see her.

'You know Colleen,' he said. 'She takes everything in her stride. I was thinking that maybe we could ask her over for dinner one night. She could bring her new boyfriend.'

Ellie spun around. 'Colleen has a boyfriend?'

Thomas nodded. 'I thought that might interest you. He seems like a nice bloke. He was at the match. Do you feel like pizza or Chinese?'

How could Thomas be more interested in dinner? 'I need details, Thomas!'

'Details like what? He's a bloke, he seems nice and he's going out with Colleen.' He stripped off his sweatshirt and his tee shirt started to come off with it. Ellie loved his washboard stomach.

'You're hopeless,' she said. 'What's he like? Have they been together long? How did they meet? What does he look like? Are they serious, do you think?' Mostly she wanted to know whether he was likely to move Colleen away from London so she didn't have to think about her ever again. She just wasn't sure how to frame that question without sounding insane and it was a little early in the marriage to play the crazy card.

'I didn't ask how or when they met, so I guess that means you can ask her if they come over for dinner. I don't mind doing the cooking.'

She surveyed the kitchen like she was seeing it for the first time – the open cabinets, dirty chopping boards, dishes and pots piled on the worktop and flour coating the floor in a fine dust. What on earth did she think she was doing? Didn't she have enough on her plate between her full-time job and her pregnancy *and* her mother-in-law? This was not the time to learn her way around the kitchen, too. That's why their local Chinese restaurant delivered.

Thomas moved to where she was standing by the sink. 'Why don't I jump in for a quick shower and then we go into the bedroom for our starters?' His hands stroked her sides as his lips came down on her neck.

'Mmm. This is my reward for burning dinner?' It must be the hormones but she'd wanted sex constantly lately. Poor Thomas would soon have to start taking supplemental vitamins.

She drew her arms around his neck just as the

doorbell went. 'Let's ignore that.'

But their guest wasn't going away. 'Thomas? It's Mum.' Millicent started knocking on the front door's frosted glass.

'Please, Thomas,' Ellie said. 'I beg you. Don't answer.'

'But she'll know we're in here, Ell. She can see the lights on. I should probably—' He looked worried, like he wanted to say something. 'I'll just tell her that we've got food coming. Then she won't stay.'

His eyes pleaded with her.

Ellie sighed. 'Fine. You order the food and I'll let her in.'

'No, I can get the door.' He made a move towards the sitting room.

But she wasn't about to let him water down her message. 'I know you, Thomas. You're too nice. You'll end up inviting your mum for dinner and I really want to spend the evening alone with you.' She grinned wickedly. 'We've got things to do.' She kissed him deeply as his mother continued to knock. Then she heard the letterbox flap open. Now they were busted. 'I'll let your mother in before she tries opening the door with her credit card. I don't feel like pizza. Order me the chicken chop suey and tom yum soup, please.'

She flung open the door. 'Hi, Millicent.'

'Hello, dear. How are you?'

The question surprised Ellie. 'Oh, erm, I'm okay, thanks. We've just ordered dinner and Thomas was about to get into the shower. He's just finished football.' She knew Millicent would get the hint, but she also knew she wouldn't take it.

'I won't stay long, then,' she said, waiting to be

invited in.

Ellie knew better than to believe that. She stepped aside.

'Is something burning?' Millicent asked, sniffing the air as she swept into their kitchen.

'Oh, I was making soufflés earlier.' She didn't mention that they weren't actually edible. Or even cooked. She was already a useless wife as far as her mother-in-law was concerned.

Thomas stared at his mum with his phone in his hand and a wary expression on his face. 'What's up, Mum?'

'Can't a mother visit her son?' Her eyes darted around the kitchen, which made Ellie wish she'd tidied up.

'Of course,' Thomas said.

Something was going on. 'Is everything all right, Millicent?' Not that she really wanted to get into any long-winded conversation if the answer was no.

Her mother-in-law's eyes filled with tears. 'Actually no, dear, it's not.' She sighed in that dramatic way that Ellie knew meant this was about her ex-husband. 'Thomas, your father wants the dining table.'

Oh god, not the dining table again, Ellie thought.

Gently, Thomas said, 'Mum, you agreed to give it to them this year.'

'But it's our family table!' she cried, practically flinging herself into her son's arms.

He rolled his eyes at Ellie over his mother's shoulder. 'It was Grandma's table, Mum, and Dad should have it. We said we'd help you find a nice replacement. We can go to one of those auction houses in South Ken to look.'

'Everything is changing,' Millicent said, pulling herself away to run her thumbs along the waistband of her long Burberry skirt and tuck in the black silk blouse where it had started to billow in her distress. 'Everything is changing for the worst.'

At least she didn't point at Ellie when she said this, but there was no doubt that's what she meant.

Thomas threw her a pleading look.

Ellie knew what he wanted. The doctor gave them the all-clear last week at her twelve-week scan but her parents were away in Corfu and they'd agreed to tell both mums together.

Why should Millicent get to find out first just because she was having one of her near-daily meltdowns, while Ellie's nice normal undramatic mother had to wait till after she'd landed back at Heathrow?

It wasn't fair, but what could she do? They'd never get Millicent out of the flat when she was this deep in self-pity. And she did really want to go to bed with Thomas as soon as they were alone again.

Her libido beat her filial devotion into submission. She nodded to her husband.

'Mum, everything is definitely not getting worse.' He moved to Ellie and put his arm around her. 'We're going to have a baby. A Christmas baby.'

Millicent's eyes widened for a split second. Then she threw herself back into her son's arms. 'I'm going to have a grandchild? Really? My first grandchild? At Christmas? Oh Thomas, this is wonderful!'

Finally, she seemed to remember that Ellie was actually the one carrying the baby. She moved to awkwardly hug her. 'You'll never understand how happy this makes me, Ellie. Raising Thomas was the most rewarding thing I ever did.'

Ellie braced herself, waited for her to say something about getting to raise her grandchild now. That would be just like her. She'd insinuated herself into every aspect of their lives. Why not raise their child, too? With the way she treated Thomas they were just a step away from being some twenty-first-century Oedipal family anyway.

'And now you'll get to have the same experience with your own child,' Millicent said, throwing Ellie completely off-kilter. If she didn't know better, she'd think it was a kind thing to say.

But this was Millicent. She turned to Thomas. 'We'll still go on our holiday, though, right? Ellie isn't due until Christmas. I have to have my holiday.'

Ellie was just about to object when Thomas said, 'Yeah, of course, Mum. We've already booked the villa, haven't we?'

She stared at Thomas. As if! He was not going off on holiday with his mother a month before she had to give birth to his child. What was she supposed to do if she went into labour, Skype him?

But it wasn't the time for that argument. Millicent was obsessed with that week away. They'd been doing it since her husband left her, always the same week at the same villa in Sardinia. Ellie thought it was weird as hell, but it wasn't the time to mention that either.

'Well, Millicent, our takeaway should be here in a minute, so…'

'Right, I'm off,' she said like she hadn't had a breakdown in their kitchen two minutes ago. 'Thomas, promise you'll ring me tomorrow? I want to know how everything progresses, and that you're all right.'

Yeah, thought Ellie, he'll be sure to tell you all about his exhaustion and cravings and rabbit-turd poos.

Week Fifteen… Blueberry Muffins

Chapter 7
JANE

'Thank god we don't have to go through this,' Jane murmured to Katie, feeling her heart thump as she scanned the busy bar. 'It was bad enough dating in the olden days before everyone started waxing off their lady gardens and Instagramming all their meals. It's way too much exposure now, if you ask me.'

She'd never been a great one for exposure. Despite her day job, she was always more comfortable hovering at the back of their group photos. Even before the children and losing her figure, she treated cameras like she did those young women who stand in malls asking if you'd like your hair straightened or your nails buffed: best avoided when possible.

Singles nights were amongst the most popular of the Curvy Girls Club events though and, to be fair, everybody looked like they were up for a laugh, with or without their pubic hair. But Jane knew how much Katie worried that someone would be made to feel bad, and she was nervous for her.

In fact, Jane had been on edge for Katie all day – it

was her twelve-week scan day. She'd texted straight after, of course, to say that it went well, but she was making them wait till everyone was checked in for the event to get the details. 'Sweetheart, is there anything else I can help with?'

Katie shook her head. 'Once everyone is here they're supposed to just… mingle. If we see anyone on their own, we can drag them over to talk to someone.'

'Like matchmaking sheepdogs,' Jane said.

Ellie rushed through the door and threw her bag behind the registration table. 'I'm sorry I'm late! I had a row with Thomas.' Her face went even redder than it had been from running.

They'd been arguing a lot lately. That wasn't the best start to a marriage. 'What happened? Is everything okay now?'

Ellie plonked down beside them, adjusting her peasant blouse where it was riding up at the back. 'I guess it's all right for now. It's not like we haven't been through this before.'

So it was about Thomas's mum.

'Well, hello ladies!'

They all flinched when Arthur, their longest-serving member and resident pain in the arse, came in. 'So we meet again!' His watery pale blue eyes scanned the room. They'd unleashed a monster when Arthur came to one of the first singles events. Before that he was a paunchy, poorly dressed middle-aged man who had no luck with women. But speed dating meant a captive audience and now he thought he was Casanova. 'How's the talent tonight?' he asked, tearing his eyes away from the bar.

'Much the same as it was last month,' Katie said.

'Here's your badge.'

'Thanks. So how are the pregnant women?' He leaned over the low table to peer at each of their tummies in turn. 'Ellie, I think you've gained the most weight so far.'

'Arthur!' Katie nearly shouted. 'That's not very nice.'

He looked confused. 'I'm sorry, Katie, am I wrong?'

'No, it's not that…'

He rubbed his tummy, a habit that made his button-down shirt expose a hairy white overhang. 'Women gain on average between twenty-five and thirty-five pounds during a pregnancy. At four months, Ellie should have gained around seven or eight pounds.' He scrutinised Ellie again as she squirmed. 'That looks about right, Ellie.'

She smiled tightly. 'Thanks, Arthur. Enjoy your night.'

'You too!'

'Ignore him,' Katie said when he'd left. 'What were we talking about?'

Ellie raised her hand. 'Thomas.' Then, turning to Jane, she asked, 'Have you always liked Andy's mum?'

Jane nodded, though she felt guilty about the smile that spread across her face. If she'd had horror stories to share, then Ellie wouldn't feel like there was something wrong with her. But she couldn't honestly say a bad word about her mother-in-law.

Even though Andy was an only child like Ellie's Thomas and could have suffered the same family dynamic, his mother's apron strings stayed tied around her waist. It sounded like they were strangling Ellie's new husband.

Personally, Jane would have hated being an only

child. It might be nice having your parents' undivided attention at three years old when you want someone to applaud your bowel movements but it's not healthy having that kind of attention later in life. Especially from a mother like Thomas's, who sounded like she had the focus of the Hubble Telescope.

The early days with Andy were hazy after fourteen years together, but Jane was sure she'd always liked her mother-in-law. She was just like Andy, for one thing – easy going, kind and funny – and she'd never meddled in their lives… not even when they'd wanted her opinion. Getting her to suggest wedding guests had been like extracting state secrets from an MI6 operative. It sounded like Ellie's mother-in-law vetted all the guests herself. Starting with her ex-husband.

'So what are we going to do about Millicent?' Katie asked Ellie as they cleared the table after the members were all checked in and mingling.

That's one of the things that Jane loved most about their friendship. In all the years they'd known each other, all the way back to their Slimming Zone days, they always sorted out their problems together. Even if they were sometimes late to the party, at least as far as Ellie and Jane were concerned. She felt a guilty little stab thinking about the time that Katie had needed them most. They got there in the end but they caused her a lot of unnecessary grief first.

'I'll tell you one thing,' Ellie said. 'Thomas is not going to Sardinia when I'm eight months pregnant.' When she crossed her arms in front of her and nodded for emphasis a thatch of curls flopped over her eyes. She brushed them angrily away.

'Have you brought it up with him?' Jane asked.

'Why do you think we rowed? He says that since the pregnancy is going so well there's no reason to think I'll go into labour early, so I shouldn't worry. And he claims he can be back in London in time even if my waters did break.'

'But that's not the point,' said Katie. 'He shouldn't want to leave you in your last month. You're meant to be a team. Let his mother go on holiday by herself. It won't kill her.'

'Every time he brings it up she cries.' Ellie rolled her eyes. 'I'm surprised she's not a dehydrated husk by now. Anyway, I'm sorry to be such a downer when we're supposed to be having fun. We'll figure something out.' She managed an almost-convincing smile. 'Katie, I want to know about the scan!'

Jane couldn't believe she'd made them wait that long. When Ellie had hers, she and Katie collected her and Thomas from the GP's surgery to celebrate with mocktails. A scan is a precious thing. Especially your first one.

'Are you going to find out the sex?' Katie asked them.

'You don't have to decide till your twenty-week scan,' Jane said. She and Andy hadn't wanted to know with the first two.

'I know, but will you?'

'Probably not. I liked being surprised. Why, will you?'

'We're not sure,' said Katie. 'It could be a boy. It could also be a girl.'

'Well, yes.' Jane nodded. 'Those are generally the options.'

'No. I mean... it could be a boy and also a girl. A

boy and a girl.'

'What?'

'What?!'

'They saw twins today,' she said. 'As if getting knocked up wasn't shock enough in the first place.'

'They're sure?'

Katie nodded. 'Two heartbeats, two little bodies in here.' She patted her tummy.

'Hey, I just thought of something,' Ellie said. 'We're giving birth to the Curvy Girls Baby Club.'

But Katie didn't look like she'd heard her. 'You are happy, right?' Ellie asked.

'More like scared to death, actually. It's hard enough to get my head around the fact that in six months I have to push out a baby, but two of them?'

'If it's any consolation,' Jane said. 'You'll be so delirious by the time it actually happens that the second one will be easy. Besides, they don't come out together holding hands, you know.'

Katie laughed. 'There's no need to panic, right? I guess this does mean we'll only have to go through all the hard work once.'

'That's true,' said Ellie. 'It'll only be really hard for the first few months, until they start sleeping.'

She said this with such authority that Jane didn't have the heart to contradict her. Ignorance really is bliss when it comes to a newborn. 'But the doctor said everything is going well?'

Katie hesitated. 'Mostly, though my blood pressure is on the high side. It's nothing to worry about but he wants to see me back in two weeks to check. And he did say I'm an unusual case. Most women don't get all the pregnancy symptoms at once. Lucky me.'

'So you're just being greedy,' Jane teased.

'I can't get enough of the nausea and I just love having to wee all the time. Plus this acne and bloating is making me feel so pretty.'

'But turned on too, right?' asked Ellie. 'I'm jumping on Thomas every chance I get.'

'Are you mental?! I feel absolutely disgusting, like I've constantly got my period. And these headaches won't stop. I haven't felt this gross since... the old days.'

Ellie nodded. 'I feel like an absolute blob, too. Though I still want to jump on Thomas.'

'Should we be worrying about this?' Katie asked. 'I mean, we've got a long way to go yet and it'll only get worse. Wait till we really start to show. It won't be easy keeping our sense of humour then. And it's taken us a long time to get to a good place.'

'We've just got to keep reminding ourselves that we love our bodies,' said Ellie. 'We do, don't we?' She didn't look too sure.

When they glanced at Jane she nodded like she meant it, but they all knew she was the weakest link.

'All right then, I'll do it,' Ellie said. 'I have a plan.'

'What is it?' Katie asked.

'Wait and see.'

Jane was still thinking about what Ellie said the next morning as she and Kirk turned up to the meeting their producers had every few weeks. We have to love our bodies.

She used to be so stupid about her weight. Not just skip-a-meal or live-on-cabbage-soup stupid, though she did that too, but proper pills-off-the-Internet stupid.

And the ones that finally put her in hospital weren't the first she'd tried, so she didn't argue when Andy suggested a therapist to try to get her head straight.

Dr Regis was great, though Jane did spend most of those first months in a permanent state of embarrassment.

'If you like your legs,' Dr Regis had said in one of their first meetings. 'Then tell yourself that you like your legs.'

'Okay,' she'd answered.

Dr Regis waited.

'What? Now?!'

She pointed to the wall. 'You can look in that mirror. Go on. Tell yourself.'

Jane soon realised that her therapist had all kinds of mortifying exercises in her bag of tricks. She felt like a complete tit but it did get easier after a while. Jane had to talk to herself in Dr Regis's office and start her day with affirmations, too. Over months they started to help, and now she hardly minded looking like a crazy person who chats herself up in the mirror. It was miles better than feeling like a worthless person who won't look at herself in the mirror.

As Jane sat in the producers' meeting her hand drifted to her tummy. There was definitely more middle around her middle now. She had to let her bosses know why, so after everyone got their teas and the meeting was about to start, she said, 'I have some news.' The words caught in her throat but she forced them out. 'I'm pregnant. In case you thought I was just eating too many pies.'

Harriet was the first to speak. 'Wow, well done, Jane!' she said like Jane had run a 10k, not fertilised an egg. 'How far along are you?'

'Fifteen weeks.' According to Ellie the baby was the size of a blueberry muffin. 'So I guess we should think about how to let viewers know.'

Harriet glanced at Susie, the other producer. 'I'm not sure that's a good idea right now. As you know, Jane, your repartee with Kirk plays really well with audiences and while we know there's nothing really going on between you two, we wouldn't want to introduce anything that might dispel the myth for your viewers.' She pulled the ratings sheets from the front of her notebook. 'Especially not now when we seem to be getting a little dip in viewership. Here, look. It's small, nothing to worry about, I'm sure, but we're keeping an eye on it.'

Kirk and Jane looked at the data. It wasn't a big drop, but it was a drop, and she knew from her producing days that it would set alarm bells ringing.

Bronzed and beardy Kirk was looking at Jane. Harriet was looking at Jane. Susie was looking everywhere but at Jane.

She felt like the elephant in the room. 'Are you sure we shouldn't tell the viewers about me? If they think I'm just getting fat...'

Susie spoke up. 'Oh, I'm sure that's not why the numbers are down.'

Jane didn't point out that she hadn't thought that either until Susie mentioned it.

'Maybe you could wear more black?' Harriet suggested. 'Then it wouldn't have to be obvious.'

Susie stopped chewing on her pen. 'How much weight do you have to gain?' she asked. 'Because I have a friend who only put on a little over a stone. We might be able to cover that with the right wardrobe.'

Jane bit her tongue. She could gain a stone in a good week on holiday in the South of France. 'You're not actually suggesting that I hide my pregnancy?' She felt her face flush with anger. 'Because the viewers will probably notice when I'm not there for a few months after the birth.'

'No, no, of course not!' Harriet said. 'Let's just get over this rough patch and then we can introduce the happy news.'

But the news didn't seem quite so happy any more.

Week Twenty... We've Got Lunch!

Chapter 8
ELLIE

The perfect solution to her mother-in-law problem plonked itself on Ellie's plate after weeks of getting nowhere with Thomas on the holiday issue. She'd given up trying to talk to him about it after he got teary with frustration at being caught between a mother and a hard wife.

But then he appeared beside her desk just after lunch. Which was unusual. Despite working for the same company they didn't usually see each other during the work day. For some reason it seemed important to them both not to look like a couple in the office. 'Have you got a minute?' he asked. 'I've just had a call from Dad.'

That was a surprise. 'Is everything okay?' She motioned him to an empty conference room, away from her open-plan desk.

He blew out his cheeks. 'Dad's left Suki.'

'You're kidding, when?!'

'It sounds like it's been in the works for a while, but he actually left over the weekend.'

'Do you think it's really over? Is he okay?'

'You know him. He never tells me how he's really feeling. I'm worried about him. Could you talk to him? Just to make sure he's okay. I don't need both my parents falling apart.'

'Of course. I'll ring him now and try to meet him for lunch or something. Are you okay?'

'I'm fine,' he said. 'Just worried about Dad.'

Thomas wasn't overly close with Suki but she had been a part of his life for almost a decade.

Had been. Already Ellie was thinking in the past tense. She laughed. 'He couldn't have done this three months ago and saved us all the aggravation at the wedding? Sorry, that was insensitive.'

'I was thinking the exact same thing. He's got a bad sense of timing.'

Hmm, maybe not, thought Ellie. Because if he was now single again, wouldn't he make the perfect travel companion for someone going to, say, Sardinia?

No, it was a bonkers idea. Just because Jack was single again and Millicent, despite her animosity, still held a torch for him… And he had tried for years to get her to forgive him, and she definitely would have if he wasn't still with Suki. That didn't mean they'd kiss and make up.

But some divorced couples did. She was sure of it.

As soon as she got back to her desk, she googled it. She was right. It wasn't a huge proportion, but some couples did get back together. So it wasn't impossible.

And bonkers as it was, it would be a perfect solution.

As she left her desk that evening she double-checked her handbag for phone, keys and Rennie (you'd think her unborn child was made of Brussels sprouts sprinkled with bran flakes). But aside from feeling nauseated and flatulent and weirdly out of breath for no reason, so far the pregnancy wasn't as bad as she'd feared. At least it wasn't as bad as Katie was feeling. She seemed to have all the really awful symptoms. Some days she could barely get out of bed.

Climbing the stairs from the Tube, she gripped her handbag tightly. Despite appearances, not everyone with a beard around their office was a hipster looking for the next cool bar to try. As they'd seen when they turned up for bingo, some were junkies who might be looking for the next unguarded purse to steal.

They could afford to have a better office these days but Katie wasn't about to leave the place where it all began. Besides, Ellie thought as she pushed open the large metal door, they'd all miss Pete.

He stood near their desks in the large space under the railway arches, upright and stern in his bowler hat. As menacing as he tried to look, he was really a big pushover. It was hard to be threatening, even as a seven-foot-tall grizzly bear, wearing a nineteenth-century velvet hat.

Rob's cousin, David, hadn't lost any of his passion for taxidermy since they'd taken over part of his studio for the Curvy Girls Club business. In fact, he was becoming quite well-known for his fantastical amalgams these days. So the bird/mice and frog/moles came and went as the trend for quirky Victoriana had blossomed, but Pete the bear had a home there for life.

There were a few other long-time residents – the

mouse orchestra, the curled-up black cat and a grimacing Pekinese wearing a tiara – as a few of his clients had dropped off their dearly departed pets only to decide they didn't really want the dead animal stuffed on their mantelpiece.

Rob ambled from the kitchen with a tray of fancy canapés. They always pushed the boat out for these meetings. 'Hey, how are you?' he asked, biting into a puff pastry that crumbled all down his sweatshirt.

She kissed him on the cheek. Rob never failed to make her smile. He wasn't a goofball exactly, just a happy chappy who saw the world as a wondrous place and swept everyone along in his wake. 'I'm great. What about you? Getting used to the idea of becoming a dad?'

'Times two,' he said, running his hands through his thick brown hair. 'It's exciting. But terrifying.'

'Well, you have had a lot of change lately. You and Katie were still in the first flush of romance this time last year.'

'You weren't far ahead of us, you know. You weren't even engaged to Thomas yet, and now look at you. Married with a kid, nearly. Yeah, a lot of change.'

'But good, right?'

'Oh yeah, definitely good! Poor Katie's really have a rough time, though.'

'Are you talking about me?' she asked, emerging from the loo.

Ellie glanced at Rob, looking for clues as to her mood, but he gave her his usual easy smile. Maybe it was a good day. 'I'm just saying you must be some kind of medical miracle. I've never heard of anyone getting all the possible pregnancy symptoms at once.'

Katie scoffed. 'Rob, didn't I say that to the doctor today? She claims I'm just unlucky. I can't believe something so tiny can cause such misery.'

'Well actually, they're not that tiny any more. They're the size of avocados.' She smiled. 'And Jane's and mine are the size of those chicken wraps from Pret a Manger. So between us we've got lunch!'

Katie stared at her.

'You're right. That's a sick thought.' She pulled herself together. 'Maybe twins means more symptoms? Double the fun, double the trouble. Your blood pressure is okay now though, right?'

But to her dismay, Katie shook her head. 'It's still a bit high. I wondered if it had something to do with my thyroid but the GP doesn't think so.'

They didn't often talk about Katie's thyroid anymore. Funny, because there was a time when it felt like that's all they were talking about. 'Will you have to have medication or something?'

'Bed rest,' Rob said, encircling Katie's waist with his arms. Katie always said his barrel-chested girth made her feel petite when he did that. Which was a nice feeling.

But she wasn't in the mood to feel petite. She shrugged him off. 'Maybe, the GP said, and only if it gets worse. Which it won't. I can't spend the next six months in bed. There's too much work here to do. Speaking of which, where is Jane?'

'I'm here, I'm here! Sorry I'm late,' she said from the doorway. 'I had to wait for Andy to get home before I could leave. Ooh!' She plucked a tiny quiche from the tray on the desk. 'I love the bacon ones.'

Katie passed around the usual photocopied sheets

with the month's accounts. The Curvy Girls Club had exploded in the last year and now they had three full-time employees alongside Katie organising events across London and the South-east. Plus Rob, who worked part-time managing their website. He'd been an honorary curvy girl from the beginning.

'So it all looks good,' said Katie. 'Event attendance is up again and Rob's been number crunching the feedback. People still love the club.' She allowed herself a little smile. 'Any other business?'

'Yes.' Ellie raised her hand. 'I have something for you. For us.' She handed Jane and Katie each a small card.

You're an amazing friend.

You're unique.

You always do the best you can.

'I think we need reminding about why we love ourselves,' she said. 'There are loads of reasons and I've got leftover place cards from the wedding.'

'You're an amazing friend too, sweetheart,' said Jane.

She laughed. 'I know.' She pulled a card from her purse. 'That's why I've got mine in here. For when we need a boost.'

'Thank you,' said Katie. 'Speaking of doing the best we can, I want to know how Jane's meeting went.'

Jane's knitting needles stilled. 'The numbers are the same. That's to say, they're still down. I did try again to broach the idea of telling our audience about the pregnancy but the producers are dead set against it.' Her needles began to fly again.

'It's not like you can hide it until you give birth,' Rob said.

'Ha! The producers seem to think I should.' She glanced away from them for a moment. 'I'm afraid they'll get rid of me.'

'They can't do that!' Katie said. 'It's not allowed.'

'But you know it is, Katie. Remember?'

Yes, thought Ellie, they'd learned that the hard way when Katie was made redundant. There was no law against job discrimination based on trouser size.

Katie reddened at the thought. 'My case was different. They can't get rid of you for being pregnant. I'm sure they can't.'

'Do you want to talk to my brother?' Rob asked. His brother was a barrister who'd advised Katie.

'No, no, I'm sure it'll be fine,' Jane said. 'I'm just being silly. I'm sure of it.'

Ellie wished she could be as sure.

Week Twenty Eight... Hold the Potatoes, Please

Chapter 9
JANE

Over the next two months the ratings kept sliding. The time had definitely come. Jane felt huge. She was starting to look huge. The show was only slightly more popular now than some of the late-night infomercials selling Hoover hair trimmers and chin toners. Every week the producers told Jane not to worry and that they were keeping an eye on things.

What they meant was that they were keeping an eye on her waistline.

'Listen,' she said, trying to keep the exasperation from her voice. 'We can't hide my pregnancy forever.'

'We're not hiding it,' said Harriet. 'We're just not mentioning it. It's not that important, really. The viewers tune in because of what you're saying, not how you look.'

This was meant to make her feel better. But Jane suspected it wasn't true.

'It's really the dynamic between you and Kirk that

they love,' Susie added.

'But how do we know that?'

'Because we've done focus groups, Jane.'

'Not since we first aired, though. Can't we run one again? Something must be making viewers switch channels. I think it's best if we find out what it is.'

She knew she was probably signing her death warrant as a presenter with those words. Focus groups were brutally honest. She felt sick just thinking about what the feedback would say. But she couldn't sit through many more of those meetings with things the way they were. 'Please. We need the viewers to tell us what's going on.'

Harriet nodded. 'We've already thought about that and, actually, we're in the process of commissioning one.'

'When?' At least Jane would know the date of her execution.

'The company who runs them for us can't schedule anything for at least a month, and it'll take a few weeks for them to get the participants and then put together the results.'

'Can we afford to wait that long?' Every week counted when it came to ratings.

'Jane, we really don't think the focus group will tell us anything we don't already know.' Susie looked sad to have to give her this news.

'Which is?'

When both producers avoided eye contact Jane knew that she was the problem they didn't want to talk about.

Harriet found her courage first. 'We think the dynamic between you and Kirk has... shifted somewhat. There seems to be less of the flirty banter than usual. And since we know that's what the viewers like, we'd like you and Kirk to step it up a bit. We've already talked to Kirk. He's going to give you more compliments, that sort of thing. It should help.'

She felt like the ugly friend that nobody wanted to dance with. Had Kirk stopped flirting with her? It was true that she felt about as sexy as an orthopaedic shoe. It had been weeks, maybe months since she'd had sex with Andy, though after so long together dry spells weren't anything to worry about. Were they?

'Is there anything I can do?' Jane directed her question to Harriet rather than Miss My-friend-went-into-labour-still-wearing-her-size-six-Channel-dress.

'Just try to be your old self, Jane.'

Unpregnant, she meant.

As she left the meeting she pulled out Ellie's latest card.

You learn from your mistakes and keep getting stronger.

Your smile. It makes other people happy.

Your achievements. You've done a lot in your life.

You've done a lot in your life, she repeated to herself as she made her way to Giovanni's to meet Andy. A lot.

It had been their restaurant since they first started dating, an over-the-top Italian with wax-covered Chianti bottles on the tables and plastic vegetables hanging from the ceiling. Amidst all the sleek and shiny restaurants in Soho it defiantly stood its ground as the unglamorously aging auntie who knew she could cook.

'Tough day at the office?' he asked, passing Jane a breadstick.

She looked at her husband then, and was so grateful for him. Through thick and thin, and fat and thin, he was her constant. Even when she was at her craziest, when she couldn't get pregnant and then when she did, she never doubted Andy's devotion. And that had only strengthened over their years together. 'I love you,' she told him.

'Well, I love you too,' he said. 'Seriously, tell me what's wrong. Is it the ratings?'

'No, I don't think that's it exactly. I just feel like I've been here before. Only last time I didn't realise it and now I do and that scares me.'

Andy's face went deadly serious. 'In what way were you here before?'

Jane knew what he was afraid of and she wished she could just bat the fear away for him. But that wouldn't be honest. 'Well, for one thing, the producer had an almost identical conversation with me when I was presenting before.'

It was just around the time Abby turned six months old when her old producer, Karen, called the meeting. Life felt pretty great up to that point.

But before Jane fully understood what was happening, Karen was talking about focus groups and sliding ratings and she was asking what she'd done wrong.

'Nothing!' Karen had assured her. 'Like I said, you've tested well with viewers in the past... Jane, this isn't an easy thing to say, and it's nothing personal at all. But you know that we're presenting a certain image on the show. Of course we understand that you've had a baby, and we hope you're getting back on track now. If there's anything we can do to help, just let us know, okay?'

Nobody mentioned the F word, then or now. It didn't matter. Sitting there in Giovanni's, Jane knew what they meant. 'I think my size is the problem,' she told Andy. It felt like a shameful confession.

'Don't say that!' he nearly shouted.

'I'm sorry, but I'm afraid it's true.'

'Jane, you are beautiful. You're womanly and lovely. And you're pregnant. It's not healthy to try to lose weight now, for you or the baby.'

'I know. I'm just saying that I'm afraid I'll lose the show, and you know how hard it was for me to do this again.'

He took her hand. 'I do know. I also know that if you go backwards, Jane, we might lose you. And I couldn't stand that. Promise me you won't go back to those pills. Or any pills or nutty diets. Promise me.'

Jane looked into his face and saw the fear there, and the love. She'd put him through so much already. 'I won't, I promise.'

The waiter brought their lunch. She was sure the grilled salmon was delicious but she'd lost her appetite.

Her phone buzzed.

Our babies are the size of a potato ☺ *Ellie xx*

She laughed when she read it.

'What's funny?'

She turned the phone round so he could read the text. 'If it's only as big as a potato, then why do I feel like the whole sack?'

She could tell his smile at her lame joke was forced. It was a little too close to the bone and they weren't finished chewing on that yet.

'What will make you feel better?' he asked.

Less girth, Jane wanted to say. 'I don't know.'

'Do you want to go back to Dr Regis?'

That woman had literally been a life-saver. 'No, thanks, I don't think so. What's she going to say that I don't already know? I need to love myself and accept myself. And I do, mostly, honestly I do. It's just hard to remember that when others clearly don't.'

'I do.'

'I know you do, and I will work this through.' She caught his look of uncertainty. '*We'll* work this through, together and without going backwards. I don't want to go back to those days any more than you do. I'll just need to flirt more on telly with Kirk, I guess, to get the ratings up.'

She risked a smile and he returned it.

'That's my girl,' he said. 'As long as you save your best flirting for me.'

'Ah, that's the difference. With you it's flirting with intent.'

He leaned in and kissed Jane softly on the mouth. 'I could take the afternoon off if you want to do anything else with intent.'

Honestly it was the last thing she had on her mind

but after their dry spell, dear, sweet Andy deserved to have the hosepipe ban lifted. 'Let's get the bill.'

Week Thirty… Dinner Dates

Chapter 10
Ellie

It took more than two weeks after Thomas's dad left his wife before Ellie was able to get a lunch date booked in with him. He seemed to have a lot of people wanting to help him through his hour of need. She just hoped none of them were trying to become her future stepmother-in-law.

Their first lunch together sparked a weekly tradition but no matter how many chances she gave Jack to talk about his disintegrated marriage, he always changed the subject. So she was no closer to finding out what happened than Thomas was. She didn't want to push the poor man. Besides, now she had her own agenda.

As she scanned her closet she realised sadly that all her clothes looked terrible on her. She'd bought a few maternity dresses, hoping they'd transform her widening waistline into the neat little bump like the mannequins in Mamas and Papas. Those plastic women looked like they were carrying footballs under their tops. Ellie looked like she had the whole team up there.

Jack stood up when he saw her enter the bustling

restaurant. He was a lovely old-fashioned gentleman like that. They took turns booking their lunch spot and this week he chose the little Turkish place that he remembered she'd liked when Thomas first introduced them.

He looked younger than sixty-two with his thatch of wavy brown hair and few wrinkles on his friendly, open face but, Ellie supposed, that's what living with someone twenty years your junior can sometimes do. At least he dressed his age. Not in granddad shawl-collared knitwear, though – he almost always wore red, yellow or brown chinos with a dress shirt and smartly fitted jacket. It's almost exactly what Thomas would probably look like in thirty years, minus the garish trousers.

She kissed him fondly as he pulled out her chair. 'You look lovely,' he said.

'I look like a tennis ball.' Her hand drifted to the fuzz she'd recently sprouted on the sides of her face. 'But thank you.'

'That's my grandchild in there, and I think it's lovely. How are you feeling?'

'Not too bad, considering,' she said, thinking of how miserable Katie was. 'My shoes are killing me, though. I think my feet are growing. Is that possible?'

He laughed. 'Anything is possible. Millicent had a terrible time with Thomas.'

She studied him as he perused the menu. Was he thinking fondly about his marriage? 'Still, I bet it was exciting when Millicent was expecting.'

'Exciting was one word for it. Those hormones are something else. I never knew who I'd come home to, the madly sobbing puddle or the dish-throwing harpy.

Every day was a surprise.'

All right, maybe those memories weren't overly fond. 'It does seem to be going quickly,' she said. 'Thirty weeks, can you believe it? We didn't even have time to plan a holiday this year. Once the baby comes, who knows when we'll get to go away… what about you? Holiday plans?'

She knew it was a clunky segue but she had to find a way to introduce the idea of him going away with his ex-wife. Surprisingly, the opportunity didn't seem to be presenting itself naturally.

'Not since last October, as you know. That was Suki's idea. To see if it would help, I guess. It just postponed the problems.'

He looked so sad that Ellie reached across the table to pat his arm. 'I'm sorry, Jack, for both of you. Is it really over, then?'

There was grim resolve now in his expression when he nodded. 'She's been seeing someone else. They're in love, apparently.'

She and Thomas guessed it might be something like that. 'That bitch! Sorry, sorry, I know she's your wife but… what a cow.'

'No, it's not her fault, really. I'm the one who's had doubts, for a very long time actually, and we've talked a lot about that so…' He shrugged. 'One really can't blame her for acting on her feelings when she meets someone else.'

Just like she'd done the first time round, thought Ellie, when she took Jack away from his family.

She'd been completely ready to hate Suki for pulling Thomas's family apart like she did, but she'd been so nice every time they'd met that she could only really feel any anger towards her at a distance. 'Is her new boyfriend married?'

'I can see why you'd ask but no, he's not. She's always felt guilty about the way we started our relationship and I don't think she'll put herself in that situation again.'

'Or another family in that situation,' Ellie couldn't help adding.

When she first started getting close to Thomas he acted like the divorce hadn't bothered him much. It wasn't until those new relationship barriers came down that he let her see how hurt he'd been by his father's departure. As much as he tried to love Suki because his dad did, the pain of her involvement in the split was never very far from the surface.

'I'm the one to blame for that, Ellie. I made the decision to pursue Suki. She's not a home-wrecker. I am.'

Ellie sighed. 'I guess it was a long time ago now and maybe you should forgive yourself. I think Thomas has forgiven you.'

'I hope so. Millicent hasn't.'

'Well, no, that's true. But she blames Suki more, so now that she's not in the picture maybe it'll be easier for her.'

She searched his face for any sign that he wanted that too, but his expression remained inscrutable. 'On a completely different topic, when are you coming to see the new flat? We're unpacked now. We'll have to move the table and chairs out soon to make room for the baby, so get your dinner while you can.'

'I'm waiting for an invitation.'

'Don't be silly, you're always welcome. Come later

this week for supper, will you?'

'All these meals. You'll make me fat.' He smiled. 'I'd love to come, thank you.'

Good, Ellie thought. If her plan worked, maybe he'd swim off the extra calories in Sardinia.

Ellie looped her arms around Thomas's middle and rested her cheek against his broad back as he ladled stock into the chicken and seafood paella. Her hands barely touched when she did that now, with the baby bump in the way. 'Your dad should be here in a quarter of an hour. I'll just get the good candlesticks.' Jack and Suki got them Waterford crystal for their wedding present.

She also pulled out the dishes and cutlery, careful not to let Thomas see how many she had.

She would have told him about her plan but she just knew he'd try talking her out of it. He wasn't really one for meddling. That's what he called it. She called it good family management.

The doorbell rang just as she was trying to get her Spotify account to play. 'I'll get it!' she shouted into the kitchen.

When she noticed the cards sitting out on the side table, she swept them into her handbag to give to Katie and Jane.

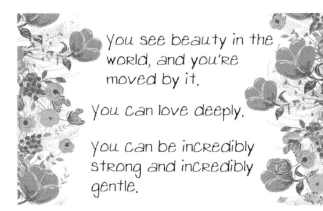

You see beauty in the world, and you're moved by it.

You can love deeply.

You can be incredibly strong and incredibly gentle.

Millicent wasn't one to go in for things like esteem-building. She much preferred to tear it down.

She looked positively funereal as usual but at least she mustered a smile when she handed Ellie a bottle of wine.

'Thomas! Your mum's here,' she sang out.

The look of shock on his face when he emerged from the kitchen momentarily made Ellie wish she'd told him. But he recovered quickly.

'Hi, Mum. Nice to see you.' Then he spotted the bottle of wine and shot Ellie a look.

She smiled sweetly. 'Sit down and be comfortable, Millicent. Can I pour you a glass?'

'No dear, thank you, I'm watching my figure.'

Of course she was. 'Thomas? Wine?'

He nodded, still glaring at her.

Ellie just caught his smirk before he turned away. 'I'll get you a mineral water, Mum. Ellie, help me in the kitchen?'

Meekly she followed him.

'Hear me out, Thomas,' she said when she was sure

Millicent couldn't overhear. 'It's crazy that your parents don't speak. It's been more than ten years. Plus, I know your mum doesn't really dislike your dad. It was always Suki she had the problem with. Besides, your dad was reminiscing about Millicent at lunch.' She didn't add that he'd called her a mad harpy. 'And we have been meaning to have them over for dinner.'

'You know that last bit is bullshit.' But he smiled as he said this.

'I didn't want you to talk me out of it.'

'And I would have, because it's a terrible idea. Does Mum at least know that Dad is coming?'

'No. I thought they should be on equal footing.'

'So you're ambushing them both. This isn't going to end well, you know,' he said. 'But I love you for caring enough to try. Just don't be disappointed when they storm out and we're left with an entire pan of paella to finish.'

The doorbell rang.

'Shall I get that?' Millicent called.

'No!' They both shouted.

Thomas hurried to the door to let his father in.

As Millicent turned to see who'd come in, her polite smile faded.

'Millicent!' Jack said. 'I didn't know you'd be here.'

Ellie tried to read the emotion in his words, but he didn't sound surprised or pleased, or angry.

Which was more than could be said of Millicent. She shot Ellie a look so venomous that even Thomas noticed. He hurried to her side.

'Well, we've wanted to have you here for dinner since we came back from honeymoon,' he said, putting his arm around her. 'But everyone's been so busy that we thought…'

We. Even though she'd dropped Thomas in the thick of it they were still a team. Ellie was so grateful she could have kissed him.

Instead she found her voice. 'Would you like a drink, Jack? I'll just get a glass.'

She headed for the kitchen, leaving Millicent glaring at her ex-husband.

Awkward didn't even begin to describe the next two hours. In fact, Ellie would have been thrilled if it had only been awkward, instead of the verbal car crash she and Thomas were sitting through. Two long, long hours of jibes and recriminations. Now that she finally had his ear, Millicent was bending it for all she was worth. What had Ellie been thinking?

'Well, what do you expect?' Millicent said when Jack answered her question about why he and Suki had split up. 'You're twenty years older, fatter and wrinklier and she's upgraded. You can hardly blame her.'

'Funny to hear you say that,' he shot back. 'When you've blamed her for everything up till now.'

'No, Jack, believe me, I've blamed you too. It's just that sluts don't change their spots.'

'Neither do ex-wives, apparently.'

'So who wants pudding?' Ellie asked, desperate for the disastrous dinner to end.

'Not me, thank you. I'm watching my waistline.'

'Is it home-made?' Jack asked. When Thomas said he'd baked it himself, Jack snorted. 'You're ridiculous, Millicent. Eating your son's home-made pudding, once, is hardly going to make you fat. You've always had a great figure.'

'Well.' Millicent blushed. 'Thank you. I guess I could have a tiny bit.'

'What are you watching your figure for anyway?' he asked. 'Got a boyfriend or something?'

He sounded almost as if he was teasing her. Ellie stopped piling up the plates. The mood seemed to shift.

Could that be?

'I do not.' She sounded insulted. 'Thomas and I are going to Sardinia in November like we always do.'

Jack looked from Thomas to Ellie. 'Are you sure that's a good idea? What if Ellie has the baby early?'

At least someone in Thomas's family was sensible. Thank you, Jack!

'There's no reason to think Ellie will have the baby early, Dad.'

'Thomas,' he said, sounding unusually stern. 'Use your head, son. How would you feel if you miss the birth of your first child? And actually, stop thinking about you. How will Ellie feel to be alone so close to her due date?' Then his voice softened. 'Millicent, be reasonable. Don't you remember how nervous you were when we were pregnant with Thomas? I wouldn't have left your side for anything in the world. And you wouldn't have wanted me to. We were obsessed with him, remember? You made me sing to your tummy, for God's sake. I'm surprised Thomas didn't sing his first words.'

Now even Millicent smiled. 'I remember.'

'Do you remember the song? We loved that song.'

'What was it?' Ellie asked.

'Handbags and Glad Rags.' Softly, he started humming it.

And then something happened that Ellie would never have guessed in a million years.

Millicent began quietly singing.

Her voice was beautiful.

By the time she got to the chorus, Jack was singing too. And so was Thomas.

Suddenly Ellie could see the three of them, before Jack met Suki and Millicent dried up into a bitter lemon concentrate, when Thomas still had two full-time parents and none of the hurt he carried later.

'Still got the voice, old girl.'

'You were a bit off-key,' she replied. But she smiled.

And Ellie dared to hope her plan wasn't quite as dead in the water as she'd thought.

Week Thirty-four... Fruit Salad

Chapter 11
Jane

'Can you move up a bit?' Jane whispered to Katie just as a parp erupted from the woman beside her. The source of the wind collapsed in giggles.

'Sorry!' the parper whispered. 'Oh my god, that's dreadful!'

'Is my arse in your face?' Katie asked over her shoulder. She scooched her yoga mat forward a few inches. 'Maybe we can switch. I'll go behind you.'

'No way,' Jane hissed. At least her arse was facing the back wall. 'How much longer?'

'About a decade,' Ellie wheezed.

'Ladies, please!' The instructor said, not for the first time. 'You're disrupting the class.'

'Actually,' said the very pregnant woman next to her, not even pretending to lunge any more. 'I'm pretty sure that was me.'

It was like a spell had been broken. The half dozen other women in the YogaBump class relaxed back on to their bums and the instructor knew she'd lost her audience. 'All right, we'll cool down now and please, no talking!'

They managed to keep quiet until she rang the gong and released the class. Ellie was the one who wanted to try pregnancy yoga like her NCT instructor suggested, but even she had to admit it was a bad idea. They weren't exactly swamis to begin with.

'I've heard that some women do yoga right up until the birth,' she said when they'd got to the noodle bar around the corner from the studio.

'Masochists,' Katie said. 'I didn't enjoy it before I had this tummy.'

Jane took a moment to marvel again at Katie's bump. At thirty-four weeks she felt like a hippo but Katie was nearly twice as big at thirty-one. 'When's your next blood pressure check?' she asked.

'Oh, will everyone just stop bothering me about that?!' She snatched a menu.

Ellie's eyes widened. 'We're just worried about you, Katie.'

She shook her head. 'I'm sorry, I know you are. But between you and my family and Rob I feel like everyone is constantly on at me about it. I've got another appointment tomorrow, as it happens. Though I know what they'll say.'

'They'll say that you're fine?' Ellie asked.

'No. They'll say I have to go on bed rest. Which is so depressing. It's not like I've even had any fun in there in months.'

Jane understood completely. Sex was still the last thing on her mind. After lunch with Andy at Giovanni's the hosepipe ban went straight back into force. 'It's temporary, sweetheart, so don't worry about that.'

'I'm just so huge. Huge and horrible.' Concern was written all over her face. 'I don't blame Rob for not wanting anything to do with me. I don't even like looking at myself.'

Wait just a minute, thought Jane. Feeling unsexy because of a bump was the woman's prerogative, never the man's. Alarm bells started to ring.

'Has he said that?' she asked with her hand itching for the phone. Rob would get her thoughts on the matter if Katie said yes.

'No, he's amazing as usual. He tells me I'm beautiful. But come on. He has to see what I really look like now. It's a fact that I'm huge.'

Jane couldn't disagree. 'Okay, you're huge. But he loves you, Katie. Don't you remember that you felt the same way when you started taking the thyroid medicine and putting on weight? I know that wasn't easy but you managed to keep liking yourself then. This is the same thing. It's not fair to either of you to assume that he's thinking dark thoughts. Especially if he's not acting any differently and hasn't said anything.'

'Besides,' said Ellie. 'It's only nine more weeks for you, and six for us. That's not so long when you think about it. Oh, I almost forgot.' She dug the cards out of her bag.

You're smart and intuitive.

You'll defend your friends and family against anything.

You bring out the best in people.

'We're getting quite a collection,' Katie said. 'Are you running low on cards yet?' Ellie shook her head. 'Good, because I don't want you to stop. They really do help.'

Ellie smiled. 'I'm so glad. And guess how big the babies are now!'

'The size of Nissan Sentras?' Katie said.

'Slightly smaller. Yours are the size of coconuts. And ours are cantaloupes.'

Jane had to laugh at that. How the hell was she supposed to hide a cantaloupe under her dress on camera? 'They're texting me the show's ratings each week now,' she told her friends. 'I'm getting a Pavlovian response to that little ding whenever a text comes.'

Katie glanced up from her menu. 'They can't torture you like that on your days off! It's like ringing someone every weekend to remind them of a bad employee review.'

Jane knew Katie was thinking of herself when she said that. Her old employer, Delicious, really treated her badly before making her redundant. It turned out to be the best thing that could have happened because she was so happy running the Curvy Girls Club, but it had been an awful few months for her.

'They can do it, I'm afraid,' Jane said. 'I'm the one who asked to be updated as soon as the figures come out. It's better to know rather than suspect I've become toxic and have it confirmed every two weeks in person. At least this way I've got time to get my pretend it's-all-fine face together for the meetings. They're doing the focus groups now so we'll have an actual answer about in a few weeks. Pssh, I can't wait for that conversation.'

'But you know you're not crap, don't you?' Ellie asked.

Jane hated to see such concern in her expression. She caused them so much worry. 'Well, something's wrong. If they haven't gone off me, then it's probably this.' She pointed to the obvious change in the past few months. 'Though I don't believe they'd mind if they knew I was pregnant. It's probably the unexplained weight gain that they're not crazy about.' She thought again about the show's raison d'être: all the fun with none of the consequences. Putting on weight was a consequence her audience wouldn't like being reminded of.

'So let slip that you're up the duff,' Katie suggested.

Jane shook her head. 'Harriet would kill me. Besides, it's not a live show. They'd only edit it out.'

She was stuck waiting for the focus group to decide her fate.

By the time the next meeting came round later that week, Jane was resigned. Or maybe resentful was the better word. And pretty peeved off, actually. Harriet and Susie had a reasonably good programme format, bar their fear of anything that seemed like real life. But in the year they'd been working together, the producers hadn't suggested even one idea to move them forward. In television, if you weren't looking for ways to improve, you fell behind. Maybe that's what was happening with the show.

'You're blossoming!' Kirk said when he saw her. 'How do you feel?'

'Like an ocean liner in dry dock.'

'Without the barnacles on your bottom, hopefully.' He laughed at his joke through the increasingly dense foliage on his face.

She was tempted to mention the piles.

No, Jane, don't be too real.

'So, the figures,' she said as soon as Susie and Harriet arrived at the café where they were meeting. The venue change had been Kirk's idea. He wanted the chance to be seen by his adoring public. He'd been on the sunbed and everything.

Susie must have drawn the short straw. She delivered the news. 'They've stabilised this week, so that's good. But we do think, Jane, that your weight gain might be the issue here.'

No kidding. 'You mean my pregnancy, Susie. I didn't get like this from eating cakes, you know. I had sex, made a baby. Like a lot of people do.'

'We know, we know,' Harriet said, clearly eager to keep everything nice and happy. 'And the focus group analysis will be ready in two weeks, so we'll know for sure what's what then… In the meantime, we wondered how you'd feel about changing the programme format a bit.'

Better late than never, Jane thought. They were finally going to earn their salaries as producers. 'I'm very open to changes to try to improve the show. What are you thinking?'

She didn't dare hope they'd let them have a few more meaty topics, but maybe Harriet could stop screaming in her ear whenever a guest made a serious comment. That would be a start. Or they could get the extra money for more live guests so she and Kirk didn't have to spend so much time talking about celebrity facelifts and wardrobe malfunctions.

'Excellent, glad you're on board with this,' Harriet said. 'So we thought you could let Kirk handle the presenting for the next few weeks.'

'What am I supposed to do while he's presenting?' When she glanced at Kirk she saw he'd already been briefed.

Susie smiled. 'You can do whatever you want! You must have a lot to take care of to get ready for the baby. Or maybe you and Andy could have a week away. Whatever you want, really. With full pay, of course.'

What? 'Are you taking the show away from me?'

'Absolutely not,' Kirk said. 'It's just for a few weeks. Right?'

Their producers nodded. 'Just for a few weeks.'

'Like when I went away,' Kirk added. 'And you covered for me.'

Except Jane wasn't going on holiday, was she? She was being banished. It felt like they were trying to convince her that her old dog was about to go to a farm while they held the syringe behind their backs.

'When does my holiday start?' She tried, but failed,

to keep the word holiday from sounding snarky.

'Next week. Kirk can tell the audience that you've gone off on a fabulous holiday. It'll buy us some time to see how the ratings do. Okay?'

'Well, I don't have much choice, do I? You've already decided.'

'We want you to be happy about this, Jane.'

She flashed them the widest, fakest smile she could muster. 'Assume I'm thrilled.'

When her phone rang a few minutes later she didn't even bother saying goodbye to them. She grabbed her bag and headed for the door.

'Jane, it's Katie.'

'I know, sweetheart, your name comes up on my phone.'

'I'm in bed.'

At least someone's day was going well. 'Ended your dry spell, eh?'

'No, I mean I'm in bed. For the next nine weeks. Can you come over?'

'I'm on my way.'

Week Thirty-six... Picnic

Chapter 12
Ellie

With Jane 'on holiday' for the past two weeks, their picnics in Katie's bed were becoming a routine. Even so, Ellie still got excited every time she walked from the Tube station to her old flat, which Katie now shared with Rob. Focussing on her friend for a few hours meant she didn't have to think about Millicent and the Sardinia holiday. Which made a change from the past month, when that seemed to be all she and Thomas were talking about.

His parents hadn't exactly kissed and made up at dinner but they were at least on guarded speaking terms again. That didn't mean Jack wanted to go to Sardinia. By the time Ellie had washed the dinner dishes she knew her plan was ridiculous. She wouldn't make the mistake of putting them together again.

But it wasn't a completely wasted dinner– Jack had put enough doubt into Thomas's brain to make him rethink abandoning her to lie on the beach with his mother.

Today, for the first time in ten years, Millicent was

going on holiday without Thomas.

He'd been sending play-by-play updates all morning. She looked again at his texts.

Just arrived at Mum's. She's packed enough for an army. Thomas xxx

As long as that army didn't include her son. She wouldn't put a last-minute persuasive assault past the woman and she wasn't about to relax until the plane was in the air with her husband still on the ground.

On Heathrow Express. Mum is quiet. She says she's ok though. Thomas xxx

Flight on time and she seems excited. She's gone to Boots for more sun cream. Thomas xxx

. . .

They're boarding.

Tears :- (

And finally, the text saying he was safely on the Heathrow Express on his way back to London. He didn't mention Millicent so she assumed she was on the plane.

Despite fighting for the outcome for months, Ellie didn't take any pleasure in it. She just hoped Millicent would have a good time away, and that Thomas wouldn't resent his wife if she didn't.

She walked down Katie's road with the woven

basket banging painfully against her knees. It was a completely impractical wedding gift, too awkward to carry comfortably, but she felt guilty not using it.

Jane answered Katie's door. 'How's she doing?' Ellie whispered.

'Mad as a hornet today,' Jane said cheerfully, leading them through to the bright little kitchen. 'Rob's just told her about the play. I've sent him out for his own safety.'

'But it wasn't his fault that those girls can't read a calendar.' Ellie started unpacking lunch on the worktop, sweeping up some toast crumbs with her hand while Jane whipped a few teacups into the mini dishwasher.

'I know,' she said. 'I just didn't want him to fall victim to friendly fire. Though she'd be crazy to shoot him. Come, look what he's done in here.'

They crept down the hall to Ellie's old room.

Ellie's hand flew to her mouth when she walked in. Rob had kept the door locked for weeks while he worked on it. He wouldn't even let Katie see it till he'd finished.

It was painted a gentle lilac with silvery-white birch trees stencilled on one wall, a few silhouetted birds flitting amongst the leaves. The cots stood side by side against the birch wall and there was an old-fashioned rocking chair in one corner. Ellie's old chest of drawers was now covered with birch trees too, and little owls. And above the cots was a giant stencil.

Play – Laugh – Giggle – Dream

'If I saw a photo I wouldn't recognise it,' Ellie

whispered.

'I know. Katie cried when she saw it. Happy tears, though!'

'I can hear you talking about me!' Katie shouted from the bedroom.

'We're saying only good things, sweetheart,' said Jane, hurrying back to the kitchen to pile their lunch on the bed tray.

It seemed so decadent to eat cheese with actual biscuits in bed. Crumbs be damned! And salads with hummus and, best of all, the mince pies had just hit the shelves in Waitrose.

Ellie bounced on the mattress and kissed her friend. Bed rest wasn't exactly agreeing with Katie – her rage at being cooped up was probably undoing most of the benefit of the rest – but there was colour in her cheeks and her shiny dark hair looked freshly washed.

She showed Katie her card.

You're not a quitter.

You give so much of yourself to others.

You can forgive.

Katie had the others pinned up where she could see them. 'Should I add it to the wall?'

'Yes, please.'

As she was digging around in the bedside table drawer for a pushpin, Katie said 'Rob's already told you about the play, hasn't he?'

Ellie didn't do a very good job of looking clueless.

'Oh, don't bother. You've got no poker face. Those dimbots are costing us thousands of pounds.'

It had taken a lot of convincing to get Katie to agree to hire the temps in the first place but they desperately needed the help with the Curvy Girls Club bookings while she was at home. 'I suppose it was an honest mistake.'

'It was a stupid mistake.'

'Now don't get yourself worked up,' Jane said. 'You're supposed to be relaxing. We can handle any problems that come up at the club. You have to stop worrying. It's a pain to have to refund all the tickets but we're doing well. We can afford it.'

Katie was right, though, thought Ellie. It was incredibly stupid to book forty-two tickets for a play on the wrong night. The temps turned up at the theatre with everyone's tickets, and only rang Rob about an hour after nobody turned up to collect them. By that point the play had started and they had no chance of getting refunds from the theatre because they'd booked all the seats a day early. Now they had to refund more than two thousand pounds. 'Jane is right. We're doing well, so even this isn't really much of a setback. Basically, there's nothing that can happen to knock the club off course. You've done such an amazing job setting it up that it will just keep ticking along. Besides, Rob is there, and Jane and I are on hand, too.'

'I know, and I appreciate that. This is for the best, I

know, for me and the babies, but I can't imagine how I'm going to face seven more weeks without going insane. Seven!' She looked miserable.

'Not likely, sweetheart. Didn't the midwife tell you that you're technically full term at thirty-seven weeks? And most twins are born early. That's only four weeks away. There! I've cut your bed time in half. You're welcome.'

Katie rolled her eyes.

'At least it's not complete bed rest,' Ellie said. 'You can still get up sometimes.' She desperately wanted to help her friend feel better. 'Some women have to use chamber pots and be bathed with a sponge.' When her gran was in the hospital a few winters ago she had a male nurse doing the job. She said that definitely helped her recovery.

Katie made doe eyes at Ellie, batting her eyelashes. 'You'd sponge me if I needed it, wouldn't you?'

'Of course,' she said. 'Though I'd let Rob dump out your wee.' She grinned. 'At least you can get up to use the loo and make lunch and stuff. It's really more like house arrest than bed rest when you think about it.'

'It does feel like punishment.' She rubbed her hand across her tummy. 'Anyone else feel like Jabba the Hutt?'

'It's the babies,' said Ellie. 'You do have two in there. And they're the size of pineapples.' She turned to Jane. 'Ours are honeydew melons.'

'Are we only measuring in fruit now?' Katie asked, picking at the red pepper hummus. They had dainty appetites these days, unable to eat more than a few mouthfuls before feeling stuffed.

'I'm afraid so. They're too big now to measure in

fun food.'

'Then I don't want to know any more,' Katie said. 'Let's just agree the babies are uncomfortably large, okay? This has been a period in my life that I'd rather forget. Other than getting the babies at the end there's been nothing good about it.'

Ellie could understand why Katie would feel that way but she hadn't really minded being pregnant so much. It was all worth it to meet her child in a few weeks. How incredible to think that just a few inches of tummy kept them apart. Oh, and probably hours and hours of labour.

'It's brought you and Rob closer together, though,' Jane said.

Katie scoffed. 'How can we be closer when we haven't had sex for months? He says we could whenever I want to, but he's just being nice. I mean, look at me.'

'Look at you being beautiful and carrying his children, you mean?' Ellie said. 'If it's bothering you, maybe we should talk to Rob about this.'

Katie laughed. 'He wouldn't be at all surprised if we did.'

'I do know how you feel.' Ellie was too big to feel like having sex anymore, either. Just the idea of hefting herself around the sheets made her want to lie down for a nap. She giggled to herself. Thomas, bless him, was still trying to entice her. She suspected he did it because he thought it made her feel better about herself. And it did. They all had nice men in their lives.

Ellie heard Rob's keys in the front door and a few seconds later the tip of a large fir tree poked through the bedroom door.

'What are you doing?' Katie asked as Rob kicked the laundry basket out of the way and manhandled the tree into its place. 'Christmas is a month away!'

'But you need cheering up and you love Christmas and I found a guy selling trees near the Tesco.' He shrugged off his coat and wiped his brow as if he'd cut it down himself and dragged it from the forests of Scotland. 'Though it probably is a bit early. If all the needles fall off before Christmas I can always get another one. You stay there and tell me where the lights and decorations are. I'll do all the work.'

The three of them sat on Katie's bed watching Rob first wind multi-coloured lights around the tree, then carefully unwrap each of Katie's Christmas ornaments and hang them. Already the room smelled of fir and suddenly it felt like Christmas. That gave Ellie a thought.

'Since the babies will be born around Christmas,' she said, 'have either of you thought of a name to commemorate that? Or is it too cheesy?'

Jane considered. 'I've always liked Nicholas. It was our second choice for Matthew, actually, so maybe if we have a boy…'

'Or Holly, if it's a girl?' Ellie said, though she and Thomas had already settled on Emily for a girl.

'You could go old school with something like Mary,' Katie offered. 'Or Joseph.'

'Or really old school,' said Rob. 'Jesus.'

'Wenceslaus,' said Ellie.

'Sherry.'

'And her sister, Hangover.'

'Very realistic, Rob. Here's another realistic one: Batteries Not Included,' said Jane. 'And speaking of batteries, Rob, do you still want to have sex with Katie?'

Wow, thought Ellie. That was direct even by their standards.

But Rob didn't miss a beat. 'Of course I do. Look at her, she's sex on legs.'

Ellie and Jane both inspected Rob's face for piss-taking. He was completely serious. 'You wouldn't lie to us?'

'And incur the wrath of the Witches of Eastwick? Not a chance. Katie knows I think she's gorgeous. I'm just waiting till she's ready.' He bounded to his girlfriend and grasped her face with both hands. 'Say the word, my love, and we'll do it right here, right now.'

'Exhibitionist,' muttered Jane.

Katie pushed him away. 'You're daft, but thank you for the sentiment. Let's see how I feel when these babies are out.'

Rob got a funny look on his face. Then he fell to his knees at the side of the bed. 'Well, then, if you won't shag me, how about marrying me?' He grabbed her hands. 'I know what you're thinking, but I'm not just trying to make an honest woman of you, now that you're carrying my offspring. I love you, Katie, and I want to spend the rest of my life with you.'

'In front of my friends?' Katie whispered.

Ellie glanced at Jane. It was getting uncomfortable. 'Ah, we—'

'Don't go,' Rob said. 'Katie, I happen to know that you were there when Thomas told Ellie he loved her, and you'd have been there with Jane, too, if you'd known each other when she first got together with Andy. Christ, you're all pregnant together. And we

109

both know very well that you'd ring them anyway as soon as you give me an answer. I accepted long ago that I'm the fourth girlfriend in this group. I'm just saving you having to repeat yourself later.' He smiled at Ellie and Jane.

'You're not avoiding the question, are you?'

Katie shook her head, her eyes starting to brim. 'Yes. Let's get married. I love you!' She threw herself into Rob's arms.

It was a little crowded with them all on the bed, but they made room for the fourth girlfriend.

Week Thirty-six and a half... The Showdown

Chapter 13
Jane

Jane had managed nearly her whole pregnancy without feeling nauseous, but one call from her producers and she felt like vomiting into the cutlery drawer.

'Can you come in this morning?' Harriet asked when she rang the Monday after Katie's bedroom Christmas engagement picnic.

'But our meeting's on Thursday,' Jane said.

'I know but we've got the focus group results. It's best to talk to you both before tomorrow.'

Jane's tummy churned. Tomorrow was their show taping day. It was supposed to be her first week back. Or maybe not.

'I've got to take the children to school this morning,' Jane told her. 'It's sports day and I'm helping out.'

'Uh-huh. Uh-huh, I get that, but we really need to talk to you this morning. We've got back-to-back meetings this afternoon.' She sounded surprised that Jane would have any objection to dropping everything to meet. The implication was clear: their meetings were more important than her family.

'I'll have to check with Andy about taking the children. I'll ring you back.' She ended the call before she said something she'd regret.

'Andy, sweetheart?' She shuffled into the bedroom as quickly as the bump allowed. He was just putting his trousers on. 'That was Harriet. They've got the results and need to talk to me this morning. Are you able to take the children into school?'

He zipped up and came towards her. 'Yeah, I can. Are you worried?'

'Of course I am!' she blurted. 'They're going to tell me it's my fault.'

He grabbed her and pulled her to him, whispering into her hair: 'No, they're not, Jane. You are a very good presenter and you know that. It's just that little bastard in your head that's giving you doubts.' He pulled her away so he could stare into her eyes. 'Tell the bastard to shut up. You're good, Jane. You don't need to be worried. The focus group is going to confirm that.'

She managed a wobbly smile. 'Thank you.'

'I'll finish up breakfast and drop the children. Go ahead and get ready for your meeting.'

She hesitated. 'There's one more thing. Today's sports day and I promised I'd help. Is there any way…?'

'I'll need to ring the office,' he said.

'Thank you! And I'm sorry to ask.'

His brow furrowed. 'What are you on about, Jane? Why should you be sorry to ask if I can help with our children?' He laughed like she was nuts. 'Get ready for your meeting and I'll ring the office.'

Her nerves were still zinging when she got to the studio. Kirk was already sitting comfortably in Harriet's office, looking relaxed and perhaps a bit smug. 'Did you have a nice time off?' he asked.

'It was a blast,' said Jane, smiling grimly at Susie and Harriet. 'So, the results are in.' She tried to make this sound light and breezy, but it came out tight and squeaky.

'Susie, close the door, please,' Harriet said. The click of the latch confirmed Jane's worst fears. They didn't want her upsetting the rest of the staff. She wondered if Susie would set a box of Kleenex on the table between them. Wasn't that what doctors did when they had to tell a patient she was terminal?

'So, we have two bits of information about the show,' Harriet continued. 'First, the ratings.'

Kirk sat up straighter, eager to hear the praise that was coming.

I will not cry, Jane told herself. I will definitely not cry. After all, presenting wasn't a lifelong dream for her. Okay, maybe it had been a decade ago, the last time she was in front of the camera, but she wasn't exactly camera-ready anymore, was she? Viewers obviously didn't think so.

She knew she could get work again in television, so they wouldn't have to worry too much about money. It had been a nice experiment but, honestly, she'd found the show's remit uncomfortably stifling. There was fluffy television and then there was *Get Happy London*. They were the lint on top of the fluff. Jane would much rather work on a show that delved even just a little bit deeper. They could have done that if Harriet and Susie weren't afraid of their own shadows.

Harriet glanced down at the paper she was holding. 'I'm sorry, Kirk, the ratings have declined further in the past two weeks.'

His smile disappeared. 'That can't be right.'

'I'm afraid it is. In fact, it's the second biggest fall since you returned from holiday.'

'When was the biggest fall?' Jane asked, not daring to look at Kirk.

'It was the week Kirk came back,' Harriet confirmed. She cleared her throat. 'We have the results of the focus groups, too, and the reason for the decline came through very clearly. As we suspected, it had to do with how the audience was perceiving you.'

But she wasn't looking at Jane. She had Kirk in her sights. 'I'm really sorry, Kirk, but viewers hate your beard.'

'What?' he said, his hand flying to his face.

'And your tan, it seems.' She handed a sheet of paper to each of them. 'You can see from the freeform comments that viewers haven't connected with the facial hair, Kirk.'

'I do not look like a paedophile!' he thundered, reading the comments.

Jane scanned the page. Nearly all the comments were about Kirk's face. *His face looks like a chorizo.* That was a little harsh, though she had to stifle a laugh when she read it. 'So it's not me?' she asked.

Susie shook her head. 'They love you, Jane. In fact, several viewers mentioned your pregnancy. It seems you weren't able to hide the bump very well.' Her look was chastising.

'Well, no, Susie, I am eight months pregnant.'

She ignored the sarcasm. 'The good news is that you

should definitely let the viewers know tomorrow, officially!' She looked ever-so pleased to tell Jane this.

Except that it wasn't really good news, was it? Because at the end of the day, she and Harriet had caused Jane months of undue stress over her appearance.

'And Kirk, if you can shave off your beard, I'm sure the ratings will come up again. Phew!' Susie grinned. 'We're so relieved that they're such easy problems to solve.'

She was totally missing the point. It was their job to guide the programme towards success. Yet for months the show had floundered because they were too arrogant to think for even one minute that they didn't have all the answers. That meant they hadn't done their jobs. If Jane hadn't kept on at them about the focus group, they'd still be blaming the ratings on her instead of old sausage-face.

No. No, that wasn't very nice. It was just as wrong for Kirk to be judged on his looks as it would be for her. The world still had a long way to go before it was fair. She reached over and squeezed Kirk's arm. 'I don't think you look that bad.'

She was so relieved that it wasn't her fault that she wasn't sure about saying more. But as they sat there listening to Harriet talk about tomorrow's running order, she couldn't ignore the injustice she felt. She wouldn't have done that to the presenters on any of the shows that she'd worked on. If the ratings had slipped, she'd have quickly found out why, instead of making assumptions. Who knew? It might be too late to turn the show around now. Harriet may have killed *Get Happy London* with her pig-headed arrogance. That would be a shame, because it was a good format, even as light as it was. Harriet wasn't doing the show justice. Jane knew she could do much better.

'So that's it?' she asked.

'That's it,' Harriet confirmed. 'Kirk shaves off his beard, and stays off the sunbed, and you can tell the audience tomorrow about your pregnancy.'

'But that's not really good enough, is it?' Jane's voice was shaking.

Harriet looked surprised. 'I'm not following you?'

'That's not good enough. I'd like an apology, Harriet.'

Susie's eyes darted between them.

'Well, of course I'm sorry that the ratings were down, Jane, if that's what you mean.'

'Yes, I'm sorry about that too, Harriet, but it's not what I mean. You've assumed that my size was the problem. You dragged your feet finding out what the real issue was, and now you're acting like it was all no big deal. That's not good enough.'

Harriet crossed her arms. 'Of course I'm sorry that it took so long to get to the bottom of things, Jane, but the important thing now is to move forward. Are we going to have a problem with this?'

'None whatsoever, Harriet.' Jane smiled sweetly. She still hadn't apologised.

The next morning as she sat in her usual chair on set, waiting for the countdown, she felt completely calm. She'd talked to Andy. They were agreed.

'Let's get happy, London!' Kirk smiled into the camera. He looked raw and bare without the beard, but at least the freshly exposed part of his face was roughly the same colour as the rest of it. It had taken several layers of foundation, though. 'Welcome back, Jane! You look refreshed.'

'Thank you, Kirk, I had a fantastic few weeks off.'

'In fact, Jane, I'd say you were glowing.' He wriggled his eyebrows as much as he could with the Botox.

That was her cue. She looked to camera before turning back to her co-host. 'Well, as it happens, Kirk, I have some news. I *am* glowing because... I'm going to have a baby.'

He looked absolutely shocked at this news, despite the fact that she was as big as a house. 'Noo!!'

'It's true.' She grasped his hands. 'Are you happy for me? Please say you are.'

The cheers from the crowd drowned out his next line. He repeated it once they'd calmed down a bit. 'I'm thrilled for you, Jane, though of course I'm horrendously jealous of your husband. I suppose there's no chance you'll run away with me now.'

'I'm afraid I can only waddle at this point.'

There were understanding groans from the audience. They were behind Jane and it felt great. 'But I know you'll love my replacement as much as you love me.'

Kirk was momentarily at a loss. 'Oh, of course, while you're away having the baby.'

'And after,' she said. 'I won't be back to present after the baby, Kirk. I've loved chatting with you every week, and being close to this amazing audience, but I won't be back.'

Harriet started screaming into Jane's earpiece. She ignored her. She knew they'd cut that bit out when the programme aired, but she was going to say it anyway.

'I'll go back to the production side after the baby.'

Kirk didn't know what to say. So Jane kept going. You could hear a pin drop in the audience. Even Harriet had stopped screeching. 'I've loved presenting the show, but I'm not naturally comfortable in front of the cameras. I find it hard putting myself out there every week. Sometimes we're judged based on what people see, and I'm not very comfortable with that. Actually, that sucks. I don't think any of us likes to be judged that way. I'd rather direct the show from behind the cameras than be directed in front of them. So that's what I plan to do after the baby is born.'

Kirk was nodding slowly. Then he smiled. 'I think you're lovely inside and out.'

Harriet couldn't take it anymore. When she strode on to the set Jane knew the cameras were no longer rolling.

'We'll cut all of that, you know,' she said quietly so that the audience couldn't hear.

'I don't care.' Jane rested her crossed arms on her bump. 'I've said it and everyone in that audience heard it. I'm going to go on maternity leave in a few weeks and when I come back, Harriet, do you know what I'm going to do? I'm going to take your job. I've got years more experience than you and I haven't made any terrible errors in judgment that have cost the programme its ratings. You know you've hurt us, and so do the execs upstairs. How dare you tell me my size was the issue!'

'I never said that,' Harriet objected.

'You didn't need to say it out loud. Your actions spoke louder than your words and I'm not about to let you or anyone judge me that way, whether I'm in front of a camera or not. You're part of the problem, Harriet. Shallow, lazy views like yours are part of the reason that so many people feel bad about themselves. You could have made a show that counters that, that tells people it's okay to be flawed, and have feelings and imperfect lives. That's what *Get Happy London* should be about, Harriet. It should be about getting happy. Nobody has to be perfect to be happy. It's about time people start getting that message. Now, shall we go back to the taping?'

Kirk reached over and squeezed Jane's hand. 'When you're the producer, Jane, you'll keep me on, right?'

'The show wouldn't be the same without you,' she said. 'And you can even grow your beard back.'

MICHELE GORMAN

Week Forty... Your Parcel is Due to be Delivered

Chapter 14
Ellie

Ellie had been lying low ever since Millicent got back from Sardinia. Far from alleviating her worries, Millicent's absence had just compounded them. Ellie hadn't gone into labour while she was away, which in her mind probably proved that she'd been right all along. Thomas could have gone with her.

So when Thomas went over for his usual Tuesday night dinner, Ellie begged off again, claiming she wanted to get the baby's room sorted.

Well, they called it a 'room'. Really, it was just the little L-shaped dining area extension at one end of the kitchen where the table and chairs used to be. After looking at the prices of two-bedroom flats they decided it wouldn't be so bad eating dinner on their laps for the first year or so.

She stood in it now with her eyes greedily taking in all the details. They'd got a builder to close it off properly with a door and it was the size of a small double room, with the cot standing against the far end.

They'd painted the walls a beautiful pale green and Thomas had found some long, shallow white shelves that he mounted one above the other all the way up one wall. Ellie couldn't wait to fill them with baby books and tiny, tiny clothes. They had a few basics already that her mum knew they'd need, and the small rattan baskets she'd found online were piled with newborn nappies just waiting to be filled with poo.

She was even excited for the poo!

Now that she was on maternity leave she spent a lot of time in the baby's corner. Or staring at the Christmas tree in the living room – their first together. It was covered with tiny soft white lights and little else, but she thought it was beautiful. They could have bought loads of ornaments from the Christmas grotto at Harrods or Selfridges, or a few of those clear plastic sleeves of baubles from the garden centre. But she'd rather build their collection over time, finding things as they lived their life together. Then each one would have a special story.

She looked at the meagre decorative offerings. The baby's scan was hung on a branch, and the sparkly white ceramic porcupine that they'd chosen together. And... that was it.

It would be a long-term project, but that was okay. They had their whole lives.

Her phone buzzed with a text as she heaved herself to the loo.

Your parcel is due for delivery today.

They didn't know how right they were, though the message came from the courier company, not Mother

Nature. She'd ordered a pink glass chandelier from Etsy nearly a month ago. They were cutting it close. Tomorrow was Christmas Eve.

The doorbell went just as she was flushing.

'Oh, hold on! I'll be right there!' she called through the door as she struggled to pull up her maternity jeans.

But it wasn't the courier with her baby's light.

'Hello, dear. May I come in?'

She kissed Millicent's cheek and led her to the living room. So much for postponing the inevitable. While Millicent was away Ellie read every one of her postcards for clues of rage. She didn't find any but that didn't mean it wasn't there. She was afraid she was about to find out.

'Would you like something to drink? I can make you some tea.'

'No, dear, thank you.'

Ellie lowered herself to the chair. 'So the postcards you sent from Sardinia were beautiful. It really is such a pretty part of the world. Maybe next year, when the baby is bigger, we can all go together.'

Millicent crossed her legs at the ankle. 'I know what you've been doing.'

So the game was finally up. Ellie considered her next move.

She could make an emotional appeal for understanding... if the woman didn't have a cold lump of stone where her heart should be.

Deny everything? She could try, but Millicent was no dummy. She wouldn't be so direct unless she really had worked out just how much Ellie had influenced Thomas not to join her beach holiday in the Med.

And now here she was, with no baby yet to justify

her objections.

'Millicent, I know you're angry–'

She looked surprised. 'No, I'm not. Actually, I came over to thank you.'

Ellie wasn't sure she'd heard right.

'It was pretty obvious when Jack showed up that you'd planned for us to see each other.'

It took Ellie a second to adjust her thinking. So this wasn't about Sardinia.

'You're very sweet to want us to be friends again and I know you did it for Thomas.' Millicent sighed. 'To be honest, dear, after so many years not speaking to Jack, I was surprised by my feelings when I did.'

Ellie smiled. Were they rekindling an affection?

'I'd forgotten what a pain in the arse he is. And he's become such an old man. I know I probably look it, but I don't feel that old.'

Oh. So much for happy families, then.

'But I am grateful to you for trying,' she said. 'I know it's not easy dealing with a mother-in-law. I never did get along with mine. She was pretty horrible… nothing was ever good enough for her and she let me know it every chance she got.' Her mouth was pulled into a grim line. 'To be honest, I think I actually hated her. I certainly wasn't sad when she died.'

Ellie couldn't believe Millicent could be so blind. 'And you don't think you're hard on me?!'

Millicent started. 'Oh no, dear, not like she was to me. She was awful.'

'But Millicent, can't you see that you've meddled in our lives from the very start? You haven't treated me very fairly, you know. You don't want me to think about you the way you thought about Jack's mother, do you?'

Millicent looked shocked. 'No, dear, of course not.'

Ellie softened at her expression. 'Then please, you have to stop being so overbearing. There's room for both of us in Thomas's life, but you've got to learn to share.'

'Does Thomas feel this way?' she whispered.

'That's a conversation to have with him. It's how I feel, and I assume you want a relationship with me, too.'

Millicent's eyes filled with tears. 'I do want that. I don't want to be like my mother-in-law.'

Now Ellie felt bad. She was just about to hug Millicent when a cramp nearly doubled her over. 'Oof!'

'Are you all right, dear?'

'Ouch.'

'Are you having contractions?'

'I'm not sure.'

'Is it sharp pain like period cramps? Or does your lower back ache?'

Ellie nodded. 'Both. Oww.' She'd had bad period cramps before but nothing like this. Her whole midsection seemed to clench. It felt more like poo cramps.

'I think you're in labour, dear.'

One part of Ellie brimmed with excitement. The other part completely panicked.

There was no going back now. Like slowly climbing the first hill on a roller-coaster, hearing that metallic click as the carriage moved slowly forward, this was about to happen whether she was ready or not. She wanted Thomas there. 'But the pain. I must be far along.'

Millicent shook her head. 'I know it feels that way, but you're not. They've just started, right? They don't last very long, maybe a minute. You'll feel fine in a minute.'

'But what if the baby comes quickly and I don't get to the hospital in time? Or Thomas can't get here? It feels like something's not right. It really hurts.' Her mind pinged with everything that might be going wrong.

Millicent sprang to her feet and pulled Ellie into a strong hug. 'Listen, Ellie, listen to me. You will be fine. We'll call Thomas. He can be home in half an hour. Meanwhile, I'm here. Do you hear me, Ellie? I'm here.'

A few seconds later her uterus stopped wringing itself inside out.

'You called me Ellie,' she said when she could breathe normally again. 'You've never called me that before.'

Millicent looked confused. 'I'm sure I have.'

But Ellie shook her head. 'Never. You've always called me No Dear. I sort of think of it as my nickname now.'

Colour drained from Millicent's face. 'My mother-in-law used to do that to me. God, Ellie, I'm so sorry.'

Ellie looked at Millicent. Not Millicent the mean mother-in-law, or Millicent the hogger of husbands. Millicent the woman, vulnerable, flawed, but also fiercely loyal, intelligent and maybe even kind-hearted, was looking back at her. 'It's okay,' she said. And it was.

Millicent brewed them a pot of herbal tea, though Ellie didn't feel much like drinking it. As it was cooling in the cups, Thomas flew through the door and went straight to Ellie, gathering her up into his arms. Kissing her face he said, 'Are you okay?'

She smiled up at him. 'I'm okay. Your mum is helping. I've had another contraction. That one must have lasted a minute or more.'

Thomas looked at his mum, who shook her head, smiling. 'About ten seconds. You're doing fine, Ellie.' She gathered her handbag and coat from the end of the sofa.

'Mum! Where are you going?'

Instead of answering, she walked to them and gently kissed Ellie's forehead. Then she kissed Thomas and said, 'I'm leaving you to it. You two are about to have your baby. Ring me with news, okay?'

Waving over her shoulder, she let herself out just as Ellie felt another contraction starting. She grasped her husband's hand.

The Curvy Girls Baby Club

Chapter 15

Thomas rang Katie and Jane on the way to the hospital. Jane's phone went straight through to voicemail but Katie picked up.

'Ellie's in labour,' he said from the back of the taxi, trying to keep his voice under control. 'We're on our way to UCH now. I'll ring again later, okay? I just wanted to let you know it's starting!'

'I'll be there,' said Katie.

'No, you can't. You're not supposed to leave your bed, remember?'

'Sod that, Thomas. I'm not letting–'

But Thomas didn't hear the rest of Katie's protest because his hand was suddenly squeezed so hard that he thought he felt a little bone snap. 'Another contraction, darling?'

Ellie nodded, trying to pant like they'd advised in the NCT class. 'I want drugs, Thomas,' she said between breaths. 'Promise me you'll make sure they give me drugs.' She grabbed hold of his jumper at the neck, painfully catching a few hairs when she did so.

'I promise. All the drugs you want, darling. As soon

as we get to the hospital.'

Katie hoisted herself out of bed, wincing from the sharp backache she'd had since she woke. They'd meant to get a new mattress months ago. She promised herself she'd order one online as soon as she came back from seeing Ellie.

Knowing that Rob would only try to talk her out of going to the hospital if she rang, she scribbled a note for him instead. As if she'd let her best friend have a baby without her!

Besides, she'd done it. Lying flat on her back for weeks and weeks meant that the babies were full-term. At thirty-seven weeks they were out of danger and so was she. Now she just had to wait till they decided to come out.

She headed for the Tube. It would be quicker now that it was nearly rush hour. Not that the post-work Tube was exactly pleasant. And the day before Christmas Eve when everyone was either pissed on office drinks or hogging seats with last-minute pressies? Nightmare.

She unbuttoned her wool coat in the standing-room-only carriage and, with her hand on her aching back, let her enormous tummy jut out into the aisle, pointedly seeking eye contact with a woman who'd piled shopping bags on the seat beside her. Unless you're about to deliver those presents via your vagina, Katie's look said, move them off the seat.

She had to stop a few times on the short walk from the Tube station to stretch her back. She'd spent so much time lying down that she must have weakened the muscles. Either that or the babies were sitting on a nerve.

'My friend is having a baby!' she told the middle-aged Asian woman at UCH's reception desk.

The woman looked over the top of her glasses, which were perched on the very end of her nose. 'She's in the maternity unit? When did she arrive?'

Katie checked her phone. 'Not long ago, maybe a half hour?'

The receptionist smiled. 'She's got some time, then. What's her name?'

Katie told her and was directed to the maternity unit.

She could feel her heart racing with excitement. And fear. Because she was about to get a glimpse of her own experience in a few weeks.

She found Ellie standing next to one of the beds in the labour suite, bent over with her hands on the mattress. Thomas was gently rubbing her back.

'What's a nice girl like you doing in a place like this?' Katie said, grinning from ear to ear.

Ellie's face was puce and little tendrils of curly hair were stuck to her forehead. 'What are you doing here?' she asked. 'You should be in bed.'

'You didn't think I'd miss this, did you?'

'But is it safe for you to be on your feet? How did you get here?'

'The Central Line. And yes, it's safe. I'm full-term, remember? Stop worrying about me. You're the one having the baby. Can I get you anything? Something to drink, maybe?'

'Oh yes, please, I am thirsty. Orange juice? With ice?'

'Coming up. I'll just run to the canteen. Thomas, anything?... Oh. Oh no.'

Ellie's face registered concern. 'What's the matter? Is it the babies?'

Katie stared down at the leggings beneath her dress. They were soaked. 'Erm. I think my waters may have broken.'

'Oh my God,' said Thomas, white as a sheet. 'Do you want to...? Do you want me to...? What should I do?!'

The poor man. As if one woman in labour wasn't enough.

'Go get someone, Thomas!' Ellie said. 'Katie, do you want to sit down?' She gestured to the empty bed beside her.

'I think I'd better not. It doesn't hurt. Just feels ick. Thomas, can you get some kitchen roll or something when you come back up? I'll stay with Ellie.'

When he'd gone, Ellie smiled, pulled Katie's arm to make her sit, and sat beside her.

'But I'm all...'

'I don't care. I think we're going to have babies together.' She put her head on Katie's shoulder. 'How do you feel?'

'Wet, but other than that, okay. Except for this backache. It's killing me.'

Ellie's brow furrowed. 'You might have been in labour for a while, you know. When did your backache start?'

Katie thought for a moment. 'I woke up with it. But I've no labour pains or cramps or anything. Do you think I've been in labour and not known it?'

'Maybe. It doesn't matter, though. You're here now. They'll take care of you. Do you want to ring Rob?'

'Oh God, Rob, I forgot!' She scrambled for her phone just as Ellie started breathing heavily.

'Could you wait just a minute?' she said. 'I need you.'

Katie grasped her hand. 'Of course I can. I'm here. Breathe like they taught us in NCT.'

She hoped Rob would be able to get there quickly once she rang him.

'Jane is here,' Thomas said when he returned with a midwife for Katie and a large bottle of orange juice for Ellie.

'She must have listened to her messages,' Ellie said. Her face was drained from the contractions. They were getting stronger.

'No, I mean she's here, in labour. I just met Andy in the corridor. That must be why she didn't answer her phone.'

Katie and Ellie looked at each other. 'Let's go see her,' they said together.

Thomas shook his head. 'Only you three would go into labour together. She's two doors down.'

'Wait just a minute, Katie,' the midwife said. She was a young dark-haired Scot who looked like she wasn't going to take any nonsense and Katie liked her immediately. 'Your waters have just broken. We need to examine you.'

Thomas looked shocked. 'Don't worry,' said the midwife. 'I won't examine her here! You're in luck, Katie. We're busy today but there is a room free.'

'That's lucky. Otherwise I'd have to have the babies in the corridor!'

The midwife didn't smile. 'We'd send you by ambulance to another hospital.'

Just as Katie thought: no nonsense at all. She followed her to her own labour room, saving Thomas the mortification of seeing more of his wife's best friend than he'd ever want to.

Jane's contractions were already less than a minute apart when Andy told her that Ellie and Katie were at the hospital, too. She registered the information and managed a smile between the contractions. Then she said a silent prayer that their births would be good ones, and turned her attention back to getting her baby into the world. She couldn't wait to meet him.

Groggily, Jane scanned the postnatal ward when she arrived but Ellie and Katie weren't there yet. Andy helped her get as comfortable as she could in the hospital bed and, with their baby on her chest, she fell into a deep sleep.

She only woke when her son began to snuffle for a feed. The hours passed in a haze of exhaustion and discomfort.

'Are you hungry, little one?' She said when she felt him stir again. She was still half asleep as he latched on. Like Abby and Matthew had been, he was already a good feeder.

'He's beautiful,' she heard from the next bed.

'Ellie! Are you all right? When did you get here?' She craned her neck to glimpse the swaddled infant asleep on her chest.

Ellie smiled. 'Only about an hour ago. Oh my god, Jane, I feel like I've been run over by a tipper truck.'

'I feel like one's been driven up my dual carriageway,' Jane heard Katie say from the bed next to Ellie's.

She laughed. 'Leave it to Katie to tell it like it is… Are you okay, Katie? Where are the men?'

'It's three in the morning,' Katie said. 'Outside visiting hours. They'll be back at eight. I feel like I want to sleep for a week, but I can't. I'm too excited.'

Carefully Jane lifted herself and her son from the bed. Luckily she'd had a lot of practice at going about her business with an infant at her breast. Granted it was a long time ago, but her body hadn't forgotten how to do it.

Ellie said, 'No, Jane, you shouldn't get up!'

'Don't worry, sweetheart. I've done this before,

remember? Besides, I've got to meet these little ones.'

Ellie looked like she might actually burst with happiness. 'This is Emily,' she said, stroking her daughter's back as she slept.

'And meet Nicholas.' Jane moved the soft white blanket a bit so Ellie could see his scrunched up little face as he fed.

'It's the inaugural meeting of the Curvy Girls Baby Club,' Ellie whispered.

'The first order of business,' said Jane. 'Is cuddles.'

Katie was staring at her twins, asleep in the cot beside her, as Jane moved slowly to her bed. 'This is Anna and that's George,' she said. 'At least, I think that's right.'

'Can you believe that they're ours?' Ellie said.

Katie nodded. 'All ours. And so beautiful.'

'Do you hear that, babies?' Jane said. 'You are beautiful. And I promise we won't let you forget that for one second of your lives.'

She smiled at her best friends. These children would grow up knowing that whatever they looked like, their strength and kindness, loyalty, intelligence, honesty and humour would make them beautiful. 'They're going to be beautiful people from the inside out.'

'Like us,' said Katie.

'Just like us all,' Ellie agreed. 'Oh, that reminds me. Where's my bag?' Carefully she opened her overnight bag. 'I saved the best for last.'

Your body.
It lets you
live your life
and it's
beautiful.

THE END

ABOUT THE AUTHOR

Michele Gorman is the USA TODAY and Sunday Times bestselling author of nine romantic comedies. Born and raised in the US, Michele has lived in London for 17 years. She is very fond of naps, ice cream and Richard Curtis films but objects to spiders and the word "portion".

You can find out more about Michele by following her on social media or visiting her website.

www.michelegorman.co.uk

 @MicheleGormanUK

 MicheleGormanBooks

 MicheleGormanUK

If you enjoyed *The Curvy Girls Baby Club*, you may also like the prequel, *The Curvy Girls Club*.

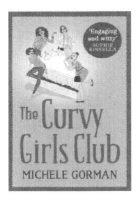

If you'd like to be amongst the first to read Michele's new books, sign up here for her newsletter.

Sign up to be first! http://eepurl.com/br8-KD

Printed in Great Britain
by Amazon